5/16

Love & Friendship

Also by Whit Stillman

The Last Days of Disco,
With Cocktails at Petrossian Afterwards

Love & Friendship

In Which Jane Austen's Lady Susan Vernon Is Entirely Vindicated

*Concerning the
Beautiful Lady Susan Vernon,
Her Cunning Daughter &
the Strange Antagonism of the DeCourcy Family*

Whit Stillman

Little, Brown and Company
New York   Boston   London

Little, Brown and Company
Hachette Book Group
1290 Avenue of the Americas, New York, NY 10104
littlebrown.com

First Edition: May 2016

Little, Brown and Company is a division of Hachette Book Group, Inc. The Little, Brown name and logo are trademarks of Hachette Book Group, Inc.

The publisher is not responsible for websites (or their content) that are not owned by the publisher.

The Hachette Speakers Bureau provides a wide range of authors for speaking events. To find out more, go to hachettespeakersbureau.com or call (866) 376-6591.

ISBN 978-0-316-29412-6
LCCN 2016933851

10 9 8 7 6 5 4 3 2 1

RRD-C

Printed in the United States of America

TO HIS ROYAL HIGHNESS,
THE PRINCE OF WALES

SIR, To those to whom Your Royal Highness is known but by exaltation of rank, it may raise, perhaps, some surprise, that scenes, characters, and incidents, which have reference only to common life, should be brought into so august a presence. Your certain desire to see justice prevail in our Kingdom has emboldened me, an obscure individual, residing in an ignominious abode, to seek Your Royal Highness' benevolent regard for the following account in which Your Royal Highness will find the Entire Vindication for those of your late loyal subjects libeled and defamed by the same Spinster Authoress

who so coldly belied
your illustrious predecessor, the Prince Regent's,
generous and condescending offer of patronage.
With most heart-felt admiration and respect, I am,
SIR, Your ROYAL HIGHNESS' most obedient, most obliged,
And most dutiful servant,
R. MARTIN-COLONNA DE CESARI-ROCCA
LONDON
18th of June, 1858

Principal Personages

Lady Susan Vernon, a charming & gracious young widow, scandalously maligned by the DeCourcys of Parklands.

The Spinster Authoress, a writer careless of both punctuation and truth, zealous only to do the bidding of her Aristocratic patrons.

Mrs. Alicia Johnson, an American exile; Lady Susan's friend & confidante;

Mr. Johnson, Alicia's older husband; to whom the great word "respectable" applied.

Lord Manwaring, a "divinely attractive" man;

Lady Lucy Manwaring, his wealthy wife; formerly Mr. Johnson's ward;

Miss Maria Manwaring, Lord Manwaring's eligible younger sister.

Miss Frederica Susanna Vernon, a school girl of marriageable age; Lady Susan's daughter.

Mrs. Catherine Vernon (née DeCourcy), Lady Susan's sister-in-law;

Mr. Reginald DeCourcy, Catherine's young & handsome brother;

Mr. Charles Vernon, her obliging husband; brother of the late Frederic Vernon.

Mrs. Cross, Lady Susan's impoverished friend & companion, "packs & unpacks," etc.

Wilson, the butler at Churchill.

Sir Reginald DeCourcy, Catherine & Reginald's elderly father;

Lady DeCourcy, their mother.

Sir James Martin, a cheerful young man of means, also maligned by the DeCourcys; suitor of the Misses Vernon & Manwaring; the Author's uncle.

Juliana Martin-Colonna de Cesari-Rocca, Sir James' younger sister; wife of Colonel Giancarlo (later Jean-Charles) Colonna de Cesari-Rocca;

Rufus Martin-Colonna de Cesari-Rocca, her son & Author of this Work;

Frederic Martin-Colonna de Cesari-Rocca, his younger brother;

Colonel Giancarlo (later Jean-Charles) Colonna de Cesari-Rocca, a hero of Corsica's war for independence, exiled to London with General Paoli.

Mr. Charles Smith, a slanderer & gossip-monger; visitor to Langford & later Surrey.

Locales

Langford: Lord & Lady Manwaring's estate

Churchill Castle: Charles & Catherine Vernon's estate; in Surrey

Parklands: the DeCourcy family seat; in Kent

Hurst & Wilford: inn & coaching station near Churchill

Edward Street, London: the Johnsons' townhouse

Upper Seymour Street, London: Lady Susan's rooms

Love & Friendship

Genealogical Table

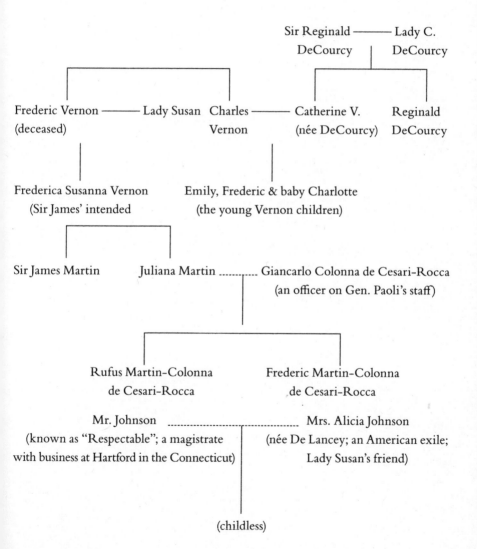

Sir Reginald ———— Lady C.
DeCourcy | DeCourcy

Frederic Vernon ———— Lady Susan Charles ———— Catherine V.   Reginald
(deceased)   Vernon   (née DeCourcy)   DeCourcy

Frederica Susanna Vernon   Emily, Frederic & baby Charlotte
(Sir James' intended   (the young Vernon children)

Sir James Martin   Juliana Martin .... Giancarlo Colonna de Cesari-Rocca
                                    (an officer on Gen. Paoli's staff)

Rufus Martin-Colonna   Frederic Martin-Colonna
de Cesari-Rocca   de Cesari-Rocca

Mr. Johnson ------------------------------- Mrs. Alicia Johnson
(known as "Respectable"; a magistrate   (née De Lancey; an American exile;
with business at Hartford in the Connecticut)   Lady Susan's friend)

(childless)

Love & Friendship

Published in the United Kingdom by Two Roads, an imprint of the John Murray Press, London, 1858

Author's Preface

"But what of Frederica?" The question is heard from all sides. Those who open this volume do so, I believe, to discover its answer. They should not be disappointed: Frederica Susanna Vernon's story occupies a major place in the following pages. I could not, however, in good conscience limit the narrative to Frederica's love-predicament. I use the phrase "in good conscience" purposefully; my own conscience is not easy. I have committed acts, omitted doing others, and said things in my life of which I am not proud. I cannot deny that the criticisms and the judicial punishments which have been directed towards me might have some basis in both fact and law. Though I am reluctant to let my own difficulties intrude on this narrative, it has coloured my judgement: that Frederica's story cannot be separated from her mother's and from the great posthumous injustice done that admirable Lady.

—Rufus Martin-Colonna de
Cesari-Rocca
Clerkenwell, London
25th of May, 1858

Part One

The 9th Commandment

—Thou shalt not bear false-witness against thy neighbour.

—Exodus 20:16

—The commandment extends so far as to include that scurrilous affected urbanity, instinct with invective, by which the failings of others, under an appearance of sportiveness, are bitterly assailed, as some are wont to do, who court the praise of wit, though it should call forth a blush, or inflict a bitter pang. By petulance of this description, our brethren are sometimes grievously wounded. But if we turn our eye to the Lawgiver, whose just authority extends over the ears and the mind, as well as the tongue, we cannot fail to perceive that eagerness to listen to slander, and an unbecoming proneness to censorious judgements, are here forbidden.

—John Calvin, Institutes of the Christian Religion

A True Narrative of False-Witness

They who bear false-witness against the innocent and blameless are rightly condemned. What, though, of they who bear false-witness against those whose histories are not "spotless"? To commit one sin or indiscretion is not to commit every sin or indiscretion—yet many speak as if it were. Such was the case of the DeCourcy family of Parklands, Kent, who disguised their prideful arrogance—indefensible in our Faith—under the cloak of moral nicety and correction. As so often with our Aristocracy, the DeCourcys did not conduct their soiling "vendettas" themselves but through the sycophants & hangers-on of their circle, in this case the spinster Authoress★ notorious for her poison-pen fictions hidden under the lambskin of Anonymity.

★ To those who object to this inelegant term—"Authoress"—it is the spinster's own. In an impudent letter to His Royal Highness the Prince Regent's librarian, the Rev. James Stanier Clarke, she wrote: "I think I may boast myself to be, with all possible Vanity, the most unlearned, & uninformed Female who ever dared to be an Authoress." This characterisation I will not dispute despite her evident insincerity in making it.

That other less prominent character-assassins later joined the cruel fray does not lessen that Lady's singular culpability. Having myself been the target of such slanderers I well know the near-impossibility of cleansing one's good name from their aspersions. And if one's name is *not so good,* that near-impossibility becomes even nearer. Whatever one answers, no matter how true and well-evidenced the defense or explanation, one is forever besmirched; even irrefutable denials serve only to further circulate the original slanders.

If defending one's reputation is difficult while one is still *of* this world—surrounded by one's papers, correspondence, calendars, diaries, and obiter dicta of every kind, with memories still lively to marshal in one's own defense—how much harder after one has departed it?

Lady Susanna Grey Vernon was my aunt—and the kindest, most delightful woman anyone could know, a shining ornament to our Society and Nation. I am convinced that the insinuations and accusations made against her are nearly, entirely false.

I have taken as my sacred obligation the task of convincing the world of this also.

Sir Arthur Helps, the great biographer of Prince Henry the Navigator, heroic initiator of the Age of Discovery, has described that Prince's not "uncommon motive":

"A man sees something that ought to be done, knows of no one that will do it but himself, and so is driven to the enterprise..."*

---

* Curiously, another memoirist, the spinster's nephew, has cited the same passage in explaining *his* motive for writing *his* memoir of *his* aunt. As both explorers & authors go on "voyages of discovery," such coincidences are not surprising.

This reflects my motives also: Having seen how an anonymous author has sought and largely succeeded in tarnishing a delightful lady's reputation and as no one else still living knows the relevant circumstances well enough to prove these tarnishments very largely untrue, the task has fallen to me. Aiding my endeavour was the discovery of a partial manuscript journal in Lady Susan's hand, unknown to the slanderers, which will, to a considerable extent, refute their vicious insinuations. *Let her persecutors and detractors quake for the Consequences!*

Churchill Castle,
the Autumn of 1794

Charles Vernon, the Churchill estate's new owner, was a large man in all dimensions and senses. In my view, humanity is always individual. We have the great urge to speak in terms of the general but ultimately everything under the sun is specific. Nevertheless, patterns can be discerned, and the sums an author might expect to gain depend to great degree on the success—not the truth—of the generalities he proposes.

In this vein I would hazard an assertion: Large men are wiser and more generous in their judgements than those of us of middle height. (Many small men are similarly generous; a combative minority has, however, given that stature a reputation for pugnacity, viz. the Emperor Napoleon. Those of us of middle stature have neither attribute, generally speaking.)

In his advanced years, when I finally came to know him, Charles Vernon's kind, sanguine temperament remained undiminished. He resembled an oak tree grown large, under the shade of whose leafy branches many could rest. He was the good "uncle" who became the favourite of every nephew, niece, cousin, and grandchild. His happy disposition did, however, render him blind to the faults of some, specifically to those of the presumptuous, haughty DeCourcys whom Fate—and Catherine DeCourcy's deceiving beauty—had tied to his (to his fate; Fate had linked all their fates).

Such benign myopia may be salutary for marital happiness, but it rendered Charles Vernon helpless in protecting others from the DeCourcys' malice. His intentions, though, were never less than virtuous.

That morning as Charles Vernon manoeuvred his large frame through Churchill's elegant rooms (his movements surprisingly graceful; many large men have this capacity), his wife, Catherine (née DeCourcy), was at her desk in the Blue Room.

"Catherine, my dear," he said, for such was his habitual endearment. "It seems Lady Susan will finally visit... In fact, according to what she writes, she's already on her way."

Reginald DeCourcy, Catherine's younger brother, was just then approaching.

"Lady Susan Vernon? Congratulations on being about to receive the most accomplished flirt in all England!"

"You misjudge her, Reginald," Charles replied.

"How so?"

"Like many women of beauty and distinction, our sister-in-law has been a victim of the spirit of jealousy in our land."

"It's jealousy?" Catherine asked. Those in the DeCourcy circle would recognize her insinuating tone.

"Yes," Charles answered. "Like anyone, Susan might be capable of an action or remark open to misconstruction—yet I cannot but admire the fortitude with which she has supported grave misfortunes."

Reginald, who respected his brother-in-law, bowed in apology:

"Excuse me—I spoke out of turn."

Catherine's look suggested he had not. A fierce barking of dogs outside attracted Charles' attention; he excused himself. Catherine studied the letter which her husband had left with her.

"Why would Lady Susan, who was so well settled at Langford, suddenly want to visit us?"

"What reason does she give?"

"Her 'anxiety to meet me' and 'to know the children.' These have never concerned her before."

A sense of grievance or resentment could be detected in her voice. I admire those people who are willing or, even more admirably, firmly resolved to rise above the slights and antagonisms of the past. Catherine Vernon was not one of them.

A Short Note, an Interruption

The reader might ask how I, a child of not more than five years at that time, might venture to recount in detail conversations at which I was not present and, further, to do so in perfect confidence of their precise accuracy.

I could explain that this account is drawn from an intimate acquaintance with the principals as well as from their letters, journals, and recollections. In several cases I have also cited the spinster authoress' unreliable account* but indicating those passages, adding my own comment as to their likely veracity. The true explanation partakes of mystery.

The lovely Mrs. Alicia Johnson, a delightful personage the reader will soon meet, once remarked, "It is truly marvellous,

---

* So that the reader might directly see the falsity of the spinster's account, the publisher has included its full text as an appendix. Omitted, however, are her earlier drafts describing actual scenes (as she misrepresented them) before she turned her account into the epistolary form affected by the author of *Pamela* and the late Fanny Burney (Madame D'Arblay), whose literary and social distinction she sought to emulate, though without success.

Mr. Martin–Colonna de Cesari–Rocca"—(despite her American origins Mrs. Johnson acquired true English poise and a distinguished formality through long residence in our country; as I am myself without pretension I use the simpler "Martin–Colonna"; of course at school this was shortened to "Colon," but I took that in good humour which is also my habit)—"your uncanny ability to describe the events of years ago with a precise accuracy that is truly astonishing. What a child you must have been! At many of these events you could not have been present."

My dear mother also remarked on this when she said, "Why do you bother seeking to make your fortune in the rare and precious woods trade when, with your abilities, you could do anything to which you set your mind? You could dedicate yourself to literature like Pope, or to history like the great Gibbon; your ability to exactly imagine former scenes and past times, despite not having been present yourself, is nearly indecent; instead you insist on pursuing the perilous and speculative rare woods trade, hardly a dignified occupation for a Martin..."

Parents, however, cannot set our path; no matter how wise their advice we will follow our own inclinations wherever they lead.

A Delightful Country Retreat, though Boring

Unlike the DeCourcys, who were proud of their suffi-
ciency, there were many who depended upon—and were
deeply grateful to—Lady Susan for her friendship. Such was
the case of Mrs. Fanny Cross, a widow whose late husband, a
substantial holder of East India Company shares, turned out to
be a more substantial debtor. To aid her friend, Lady Susan
proposed that Mrs. Cross accompany her to Churchill, making a journey which could have been tedious, pleasant for them
both.

"My brother-in-law, Charles Vernon, is very rich," Susan
said as the carriage jostled along the Surrey road. "Once a man
gets his name on a Banking House, he rolls in money. So, it is
not very rational for his lady to begrudge the sums he has
advanced me."

"Decidedly irrational," agreed Mrs. Cross.* "Not rational
at all."

"I have no money—and no husband—but in one's plight

---

* For these events I had the later recollections of Mrs. Cross herself.

they say is one's opportunity. Not that I would ever want to think in opportunistic terms—"

"Certainly not. Never."

Churchill Castle lay on slightly elevated ground, though not what would normally be considered a hill.

"Churchill, coming into view, your Ladyship!" the coachman called.

Lady Susan leaned forward to get a glimpse of the magnificent ancient castle as it appeared from behind the now-russet greenery.

"Heavens!" she exclaimed. "What a bore..."

Mrs. Cross followed her look: "Yes, *decidedly* boring."*

For visitors to southwest Surrey, then still quite rustic, there were few more welcoming sights than Charles Vernon descending the castle's stairs, his face illuminated with the most cordial of expressions, holding by hand two of his young brood.

The greetings were affectionate, Mrs. Cross introduced, and the children—little Emily and littler Frederic—entranced with their beautiful aunt. But a cloud passed over the pair's arrival when the footmen deposited Mrs. Cross' trunk, not in the main residence, but in the servants' wing. Mrs. Cross had been mistaken as Lady Susan's maid; the embarrassment for that agreeable lady was immense.

Wilson, Churchill's butler, quickly sought to set matters right. "Mrs. Cross is the friend of Lady Susan and should be lodged in the adjoining room," he instructed the footmen.

Embarrassment was assuaged, the rooms conveniently

---

* The etymological scholar Hendrik Post has caught me out here. The term "boring" was not so used in the last century. The word then was "borish," which is too easily confused with "boorish." I hope it has not been *tedious* of me to clarify this point.

arranged with Mrs. Cross taking the small bedchamber adjacent Lady Susan's rooms. That Mrs. Cross visited Churchill as Lady Susan's friend, not her servant, was thus made clear to everyone. For Mrs. Cross, however, being helpful was an avocation; it was her pleasure to unpack Lady Susan's trunk and care for her clothes. While she did, Lady Susan—an enemy to indolence also—attended to her jewels. Conversation, meanwhile, made their tasks congenial.

"I've no reason to complain of Mr. Vernon's reception," Susan observed, "but I'm not entirely satisfied with his lady's."

"No," Mrs. Cross agreed.

"She's perfectly well-bred—surprisingly so—but her manner doesn't persuade me she's disposed in my favour. As you certainly noticed I sought to be as amiable as possible—"

"Exceptionally amiable," Mrs. Cross said. "In fact entirely charming—excuse me for saying so—"

"Not at all—it's true. I wanted her to be delighted with me—but I didn't succeed."

"I can't understand it."

"It's true that I've always detested her. And that, before her marriage, I went to considerable lengths to prevent it. Yet it shows an illiberal spirit to resent for long a plan which didn't succeed."

"Decidedly illiberal," Mrs. Cross said. "Not liberal at all."

"My opposing her marriage—and later preventing her and Charles' buying Vernon Castle—perhaps gave her an unfavourable impression of me. But I've found that where there's a disposition to dislike, a pretext will soon be found."

"You mustn't reproach yourself—"

"I shan't—the past is done. My project will be the children. I already know a couple of their names and have decided to attach myself to young Frederic in particular, taking him on my lap and sighing over him for his dear Uncle's sake—"

A knock on the door interrupted these confidences.

Wilson, the butler, entered and bowed: "Mrs. Vernon's compliments, your Ladyship. She asks if you and Mrs. Cross would join her for tea?"

"With pleasure," Susan replied, casting a quick look to Mrs. Cross.

"Mrs. Cross would prefer her repose—but thank Mrs. Vernon. I will join her directly."

A Scarlet Gash in the Gold Room

Even at great houses with many rooms one usually becomes the favoured spot for gathering. At Churchill that was the spacious Gold Room, decorated in opulent banker style, its colour a dark shade of yellow. While Catherine Vernon occupied herself with the tea service she also lent an ear as Lady Susan chatted with and praised young Frederic two doors away.

"Yes, Frederic," Susan was saying, "I see you have quite an appetite: You will grow tall and handsome like your uncle—and father."

Catherine approached just as little Frederic toyed precariously with the jam pot.

"Frederic, be careful!" she called.

The pot fell with a clatter, immediately followed by Susan's pleasant laugh. She reappeared, holding up part of her dress skirt bearing a gash of red jam.

"I'm so sorry!" Catherine said.

"Not at all…Such a family resemblance—it rather moves me."

"You'll want to change—"

"Oh, no, we'll have our tea while it's warm," Susan said as

she led the way to the tea table. "Mrs. Cross is a genius with fabrics."

"Are you sure?"

"Oh, yes!"

Lady Susan had the delightful quality of being nearly always in good humour, no matter the circumstances. Once seated she smoothly draped a tea napkin over the jam stain while politely changing the subject.

"How much Frederic reminds me of his dear uncle!"

"You think there's a resemblance?"

"Yes, remarkable—the eyes..."

"Weren't Frederic Vernon's eyes brown?"

"I refer to the shape and slope of the brow..."

"Oh."

"I must thank you for this visit; I am afraid the short notice must have come as a surprise."

"Only because I understood you to be so happily settled at Langford."

"It's true—Lady Manwaring★ and her husband made me feel welcome. But their frank dispositions led them often into society. I might have tolerated such a life at one time. But the loss of a husband such as Mr. Vernon is not borne easily. To stay with you here, at your charming retirement"—with a lovely turn of the head she glanced out the window—"became my fondest wish..."

"I was glad to have the chance to meet."

"Might I confide something?" asked Susan. "Langford was not ideal for my daughter. Her education has been neglected,

---

★ Pronounced "Mannering," the "w" silent.

for which I fault myself: Mr. Vernon's illness prevented my paying her the attention both duty and affection required. I have therefore placed her at the excellent school Miss Summers keeps."

"I trust Frederica will visit soon."

"A visit, as delightful as that might be, would represent so many days and hours deducted from the Grand Affair of Education—and I'm afraid Frederica can't afford such deductions."

"But she'll come for Christmas—"

"Alas, no," Susan continued. "Miss Summers can only give her the concentrated attention she needs then." Lifting the napkin, Susan glanced at the jam stain.

"I'm so sorry," Catherine repeated.

"Not at all! If you'll excuse me, I'll give my dress to Mrs. Cross, who, once rested, craves activity."

Susan rose, holding the fabric delicately. "When Mrs. Cross has applied her genius to it I'm afraid all trace of little Frederic's interesting design will disappear."

★ ★ ★ ★ ★ ★

The next morning Catherine Vernon wrote to her mother in a changed tenor:

I must confess, dear Mother, against my every Inclination, that I have seldom seen so lovely a Woman as Lady Susan. She is delicately fair, with fine grey eyes & dark eyelashes; & from her appearance one would not suppose her more than five & twenty, tho' she must in fact be ten years older. I was certainly not disposed to admire her, tho' always hearing she was beautiful; but I cannot help feeling that she possesses an uncommon union of Symmetry, Brilliancy, & Grace. Her address to me was so gentle, frank, & even affectionate, that, if I had not known how much she has always disliked me for marrying Mr. Vernon, I should have imagined her an attached friend.

That Catherine Vernon might write of Lady Susan so fairly and honestly must raise an alarm as to her true intention, her ultimate purpose.

One is apt, I believe, to connect assurance of manner with coquetry, & to expect that an impudent address will naturally attend an impudent mind; at least I was myself prepared for an improper degree of confidence in Lady Susan; but her Countenance is absolutely sweet, & her voice & manner winningly mild.

I am sorry it is so, for what is this but Deceit? Unfortunately, one knows her too well. She is clever & agreeable, has all that knowledge of the world which makes conversation easy, & talks very well with a happy command of Language, which is too often used, I believe, to make Black appear White.

Here one finds a prime example of "the DeCourcy Reversal"—a conclusion bearing no relation to the argument which comes before, marked above all by malice.

★ ★ ★ ★ ★ ★

Meanwhile, in Lady Susan's rooms, her friend Mrs. Cross found the jam stain harder to remove than anticipated. Lady

Susan loyally supported Mrs. Cross' efforts with her presence. Perusing some correspondence she had neglected, Lady Susan caught her breath.

"Something troubling?" Mrs. Cross asked.

"Yes, very much so—the bill for Miss Summers' school. The fees are far too high to even think of paying—so, in a sense, it's an economy..."

Mr. Reginald DeCourcy, Confounded

Returned early from hunting with the Lymans in Sussex, while shaking off the journey's chill, Reginald DeCourcy inquired about his sister's celebrated guest:

"Is she as beautiful as they say? I confess to great curiosity to know this Lady and see first-hand her bewitching powers."

"You worry me, Reginald."

"No need for worry. It is only that I understand Lady Susan to possess a degree of captivating deceit which might be pleasing to detect."

"You truly worry me."

"Good evening!"

Lady Susan, descending the staircase, stopped to greet them, with Mrs. Cross just behind her. Reginald and Catherine looked strangely surprised.

"What charming expressions!"

Catherine recovered first: "Susan, let me introduce my brother, Reginald DeCourcy. Reginald, may I present Frederic Vernon's widow, Lady Susan, and her friend Mrs. Cross."

After a polite nod to Mrs. Cross, Reginald addressed Susan:

"I am pleased to make your acquaintance—your renown precedes you."

"I'm afraid the allusion escapes me," she replied coolly.

"Your reputation as an ornament to our Society."

"That surprises me. Since the great sadness of my husband's death I have lived in nearly perfect isolation. To better know his family, and further remove myself from Society, I came to Churchill—not to make new acquaintance of a frivolous sort. Though of course I am pleased to know my sister's relations."

Lady Susan and the ladies continued to the Gold Room, leaving Reginald free to consider her remarks.

★ ★ ★ ★ ★ ★ ★

Over the following weeks and days Lady Susan and Reginald DeCourcy found themselves often in each other's company, to such a degree that it seemed this might have been their conscious choice. They strolled through the Churchill shrubbery and rode horseback up its downs. Wherever they were within Catherine Vernon's vicinity they could count on being spied upon. Every garden walk or chance conversation she monitored with mounting suspicion. In her mind she was only seeking to protect her younger brother's heart from a wicked temptress. Certainly Reginald DeCourcy was in many ways a callow youth, but did he require his sister's protection? Those whose malice is most apparent to others are often precisely those most convinced of their own virtue. Their machinations are ever in defense of worthy objectives, or the prevention of The Bad. But, in truth, for the Catherine Vernons of this world, the spreading of worry and discord is their true delight. An expression has it that "misery loves company." Of its truth I am not certain but "misery-causing" most definitely loves accompaniment. In this spirit—that of sounding alarm and provoking discord—she wrote to her mother at Parklands:

> ...I am, indeed, provoked at the artifice of this unprincipled Woman. What stronger proof of her dangerous abilities can be given than this perversion of Reginald's judgement, which when he entered the house was so against her? I did not wonder at his being much struck by the gentleness & delicacy of her Manners; but when he mentions her of late it has been in terms of extraordinary praise; & yesterday he actually said that he could not be surprised at any effect produced on the heart of Man by such Loveliness & such Abilities; & when I lamented, in reply, her notorious history, he observed that whatever might have been her errors, they were to be imputed to her neglected Education & early Marriage, & that she was altogether a wonderful Woman...

Mrs. Cross, who also noticed the time Lady Susan and Reginald spent in each other's company—she sometimes paused from her tasks to observe the two walking in Churchill's gardens—was not so arrogant as to presume to know their private feelings, let alone cast malicious aspersions.

"I take it you are finding Mr. DeCourcy's society more pleasurable," she lightly observed as Lady Susan returned from one such outing.

"To some extent...At first his conversation betrayed a sauciness and familiarity which is my aversion—but since I've found a quality of callow idealism which rather interests me. When

I've inspired him with a greater respect than his sister's kind offices have allowed, he might, in fact, be an agreeable flirt."

"He's handsome, isn't he?"

Susan considered the question.

"Yes, but in a calf-like way—not like Manwaring...Yet I must confess that there's a certain pleasure in making a person, pre-determined to dislike, instead acknowledge one's superiority...How delightful it will be to humble the pride of these pompous DeCourcys!"

A Perjurer's Tale

One afternoon that week Reginald rode to Hurst & Wilford to see off his friend Hamilton, who was stopping there on his way to Southampton. The old friends—if that term can apply to such young men—shared a meal and a bottle of Mr. Wilford's second-best claret. The occasion was Hamilton's posting to Lt. Colonel Wesley's forces (he later reverted to "Wellesley") in the United Provinces before their defeat by the French.

Another patron at the inn, Mr. Charles Smith, noticed the young men and, when their first bottle was finished, asked Wilford to send over a second, but of his best vintage. This Smith, aware that Lady Susan was a guest at Churchill, had a particular interest in making Reginald's acquaintance: Like Lady Susan, he had recently visited Langford, the Staffordshire estate that Lord and Lady Manwaring had acquired following their marriage, and thought to repay their hospitality by maligning another of their guests. After Hamilton departed Smith began, speaking with that knowing, confiding, insinuating tone used by slanderers everywhere.

"I was not unaware of Lady Susan Vernon's reputation before arriving at Langford—having been taught to consider her a distinguished flirt." To this initial sally Reginald made no reply, as it matched the prejudicial view he also had earlier held.

But Smith did not leave matters there: "Over the course of my stay, her conduct showed that she does not confine herself to that sort of honest flirtation which satisfies most of her sex. Rather, she aspires to the more delicious gratification of making a whole family miserable."

This did offend Reginald, who forcibly protested. A third bottle of claret was ordered; Smith made a show of poking his nose over the glass as if the intelligence so gained would supersede that for which others rely on the tongue—but that instrument Smith reserved primarily for slander:

"By her behaviour to Lord Manwaring, Lady Susan gave jealousy and wretchedness to his wife, and by her attentions to Sir James Martin—a young man previously attached to Lord Manwaring's sister Maria—she deprived that amiable girl of her lover. So, without even the charm of youth, Lady Susan engaged at the same time, and in the same house, the affections of two men, who were neither of them at liberty to bestow them."

Reginald, red-faced, argued and denied, but as Lady Susan had spoken little of her time at Langford, except for mentions of her friendship with Lady Manwaring and her husband, he had little information with which to counter Smith's calumnies. Finally convinced, mendacity carried the day, as often it will, and Reginald's belief in Lady Susan was shaken. Catherine Vernon rejoiced and was about to write her mother. But Smith, despite a feigned admiration for Lady Susan's "great abilities," gravely underestimated them. She was not to be traduced by such a scoundrel.

After Reginald had given her the particulars of his indict-
ment, Lady Susan inquired, "Were you not aware what species
of man such a teller of tales might be? The sort who makes
indecent advances to a widow still in mourning, under the
roof of mutual friends, using language and expressions that
any honourable woman would find as abhorrent as shocking;
who, when unequivocally rebuffed, then resorts to the revenge
of a cad, seeking to impugn the reputation of the Lady whose
person he was not allowed to sully!"

Within a week Mr. Smith had become a pariah in that
district; he left, evading threats of prosecution, and never
returned.

December: Parklands

Parklands, the ancestral home of the DeCourcy family, was known for the striking beauty of its Palladian exterior, thoroughly belied by the nastiness of the family within. Sir Reginald DeCourcy, the patriarch and perhaps least objectionable member of that detestable clan, was still the sort of cantankerous and insensible country baronet too-kindly portrayed in the literature of our day. Though he did not go out of his way to cause others misery, exorbitant family pride went far towards a similar result.

For weeks Sir Reginald had keenly anticipated his son's long-delayed return, as well as the Vernons' seasonal visit, so the arrival of a letter in Catherine's hand was of particular interest to him. Lady DeCourcy, however, was the addressee and she had lingered abed that morning in the hope of rendering a mild ague even milder. So Sir Reginald carried the letter to her there and watched attentively as she unfolded its pages.

"I hope Catherine arrives soon," Lady DeCourcy sighed. "The season's cheerless without the children." She tried to

focus on her daughter's handwriting, always difficult to decipher but with watery eyes especially so.

"I'm afraid this cold has affected my eyes."

"Save your eyes, my dear—I'll read for you."

"No, that's all right—"

"I insist. You must rest." Sir Reginald opened his specta-
cles★ and picked up the letter.

"Now let's see..."

Sir Reginald read to himself for a bit before beginning.

"Catherine hopes you are well...She asks most particularly that you give me her love."

He turned to Lady DeCourcy expectantly.

"Yes, and...?" she said.

Sir Reginald returned to the letter, which began with
unwelcome news.

"Reginald has decided to stay at Churchill to hunt with
Charles! He cites the 'fine open weather.'"

Sir Reginald turned to look out the window.

"What nonsense! The weather's not open at all."

"Maybe it is there, or was when she wrote...Could you
just read, my dear?"

"What?"

"The words."

"Verbatim?"

"Yes—some of Catherine's voice will be in them."

"You're not too tired?"

"No. What does she write?"

★ An innovation in that period: Though reading glasses originated in
Thirteenth-Century Italy, spectacles as we now know them, with attachments passing over the ears, were an English invention of the last century.

"Is something worrying you?"

"I believe my eyes have cleared," Lady DeCourcy said. "I'll read it."

"No, I'll read each word, comma, and dash if that's what you wish! Here," he resumed reading: *"'I grow deeply uneasy (comma) my dearest Mother (comma) about Reginald (comma) from witnessing the very rapid increase of her influence (semi-colon)—'"*

"Just the words, please."

"No punctuation at all? All right, much easier: *'He and Lady Susan are now on terms of the most particular friendship, frequently engaged in long conversations together.'* Lady Susan?"

"Lady Susan has been visiting Churchill."

"Lady Susan Vernon?"

"Yes."

"How could Reginald engage in conversations with Lady Susan Vernon? Conversations that are"—he studied the letter—"*'long.'* What would they talk about?"

"My eyes have definitely cleared. I'll read it myself. Don't trouble yourself..."

"If my son and heir is involved with such a lady I must trouble myself!"

Sir Reginald now read in a tone of frank alarm: *"'How sincerely do I grieve she ever entered this house! Her power over him is boundless. She has not only entirely effaced his former ill-opinion but persuaded him to justify her conduct in the most passionate of terms.'"*

Sir Reginald put the letter down and removed his spectacles.

"I must go—"

"No—I'll write—"

"If this is happening now, there's no time."

Sir Reginald bolted up to prepare for the journey.

* * * * *

Reginald DeCourcy was stunned to receive his father's summons to meet him at Hurst & Wilford. What could explain such strangeness? Sir Reginald's aversion to travel was well-known; he preferred to remain on his own land always. Also surprising was the call to meet at Hurst & Wilford, rather than Churchill directly. Reginald had seen enough that autumn to suspect his sister's meddling. So, he rode to the inn partly resenting his sister's interference, imagining remonstrating with her for it, but partly oppressed by awareness of his own unfulfilled filial obligations.

Arriving at the inn, Reginald found his father nearly alone in the main room, standing with his back to the fire warming himself.

"Father! How extraordinary for you to be here..."

Sir Reginald made no reply.

"You are in good health, I trust. How is Mother?"

Sir Reginald continued silently by the fire.

"What brings you here?"

With a sort of grunt Sir Reginald motioned for Reginald to sit and then did so himself, flipping up his tail coat as he settled on the chair.

"I won't dissemble and say I have business in this district," he began. "What I've come about is far more important."

"What could be of such importance?"

Unaccustomed to interrogation, Sir Reginald had no inclination to encourage the habit by replying.

"I know that young men don't admit inquiry into affairs of the heart but—as the sole son of an ancient family—you must know your conduct is most interesting to us. In the matter of marriage especially, everything's at stake—your happiness, ours, the credit of our family name, its very survival—"

"But Father—"

"Hear me out: I know you would not deliberately form an engagement without informing us, but I cannot help fear that you'll fall into an obligation which everyone near you must oppose."

"What do you mean, Sir?"

"Perhaps the attention Lady Susan now pays you arises only from vanity—or from the wish of gaining the admiration of a man whom she must imagine to be prejudiced against her. It is more likely, however, that she aims at something farther. I understand that Lady Susan might naturally seek an alliance advantageous to herself, but her age alone should—"

"Father, you astonish me!"

"What surprises you?"

"Imputing such ambitions to Lady Susan: She would never think of such a thing! Even her enemies grant her excellent understanding. My sole interest has been to enjoy the lively conversation of a superior lady; but Catherine's prejudice is so great—"

"Prejudice? Lady Susan's neglect of her late husband, her extravagance and dissipation, her encouragement of other men, were so notorious—"

"Stop, Sir! These are vile calumnies. I could explain each but will not so dignify them. I know you spend little time in Society—"

"None."

"Should you have frequented it more you'd know the astonishing degree of vile, hateful jealousy in our country—"

"Do not deprecate our country, Sir!...I don't wish to work on your fears but on your sense and affection. I can't prevent your inheriting the family estate, and my ability to distress you during my life would be a species of revenge to which I should hardly stoop—"

"Father, this is unnecessary—"

"No, let me continue. A permanent connection between you and Lady Susan Vernon would destroy every comfort of our lives: It would be the death of the honest pride with which we've always considered you—we'd blush to see you, to hear of you, to think of you."

"Father, with the utmost humility let me say that what you imagine is...impossible."

* * * * *

Reginald returned from the interview agitated and outraged by his sister's tale-bearing. She had needlessly poisoned the elder DeCourcys' peace of mind and tranquility; such is the bitter fruit which malicious gossips sow.

Reginald had resolved to remonstrate with Catherine upon his return but, in the eventuality, had little chance to do so. The arrival of a letter that morning put the house in an uproar. *"But what of Frederica?"* The reader might at this point well ask; the beginning of an answer is close to hand. Among that morning's letters was one from Frederica's school. Lady Susan assumed it to be another dunning notice for the school's hardly moral fees, but Miss Summers had written about another matter.

"No!" Lady Susan suddenly exclaimed.

Catherine, engaged in her needlework, looked up with concern.

"I can't believe it!" Susan said. "It...defies comprehension!"

"What?" Reginald asked.

"Frederica has run away!...Run away from school!"

"How terrible! Where to?"

"They don't know."

"She's lost?"

"No—they detected her plan early enough to intercept her. But what folly! Where could she have thought of going?"

"Surely, here," Reginald ventured.

"No, this is the last place she'd come; I mean, rather—"

"But," Catherine interposed, "she must miss you terribly—"

"Certainly. I just don't think Churchill would be her object. Her sole acquaintances are the Clarkes in Staffordshire—but the danger of such a journey!"

She resumed reading.

"This is outrageous! Miss Summers requires that Frederica be removed from school! No! This will not stand!...Perhaps Miss Summers is under the impression that, as a widow without fortune, I may be bullied. She's evidently forgotten: Frederica is a Vernon!"

Susan looked to them.

"Charles must set this right: Confronted with his imposing worth, even the mistress of a school must be persuaded to act rightly!"

* * * * *

For Lady Susan any London trip, even one on such an urgent basis, also meant seeing her intimate confidante Mrs. Alicia Johnson (whom I have mentioned earlier). The amity of these two ladies was a monument to that particular capacity for friendship enjoyed by women of sensibility.

(Regrettably, their candid and humourous conversations

would provide fuel for their later vilification at the hand of the spinster authoress. Perhaps we all have a spinster authoress in our lives, even if just that inner demon who mocks and denigrates all we do.)

Lady Susan's sympathy for Alicia was great. First, Alicia Johnson was an American. Her family was on the losing side of that bloody skirmish, the American War of Independence, which at its essence was a matter of larceny, grand and petty, rather than of the sonorous Defense of Rights usually claimed. Crown property, colonial revenue, and finally an entire country were to be purloined by an odious clique of disloyal Whig adventurers. At school we dismissed the Empire's loss of its American colonies with a familiar formulation, "good riddance of bad rubbish," but for those who lost homes, fortunes, and homeland the defeat remained an open wound.

Alicia Johnson descended from the Connecticut branch of the prominent De Lancey family who had chosen loyalty to King, Country, and the great British Constitution.* Their links across the Atlantic had been and remained strong: Alicia's uncle, James De Lancey (later Chief Justice and Lieutenant Governor of the Province of New-York), and her cousin, James, had both studied at Eton and Corpus Christi, Cambridge, then read law at Lincoln's Inn. For the De Lanceys the destruction of the great equestrian statue** of King George at

---

* A magnificent heritage of laws and traditions that have guided the greatest of nations and, now, empires, not a written document like the tedious & literal American one (which might, though, be suited to that people).
** According to Whig legend this statue, cast of lead, was cut up and melted down to make 42,088 musket balls; such an exact count might normally be questioned, but those familiar with the colonial Whigs' petty character and ludicrous penny-pinching, which had for decades frustrated sound administration, consider it plausible.

Bowling Green in New-York, pulled down by a vicious mob in 1776, came as a frightful shock. With the war's catastrophic denouement at Yorktown five years later—only after, it should be noted, the royal navies of Bourbon France and Spain altered the balance in the rebels' favour—many of the loyalists, who came disproportionately from the colonies' best families, chose exile. The destinations would be the West Indies, Halifax, or elsewhere in the province of Canada, but for the De Lanceys a return to London was the natural course.

Though her cousins had many English connections, Alicia De Lancey, then seventeen years old, had few on which to rely. Arriving in London during the great wave of emigration, she found her cousins' English circle grown less than welcoming. Only her father's business partner, Mr. Johnson, a gentleman with extensive interests in the Connecticut, took a certain interest, a certain interest which led to certain intentions. Older than Alicia and lacking her vivacity and wit, he had still been able to make himself sufficiently charming to persuade her to be his wife. However, over the years, their union had not been fruitful and, what was most unfair, Mr. Johnson appeared to blame his wife for the deficiency. In truth it is impossible in such cases to ascribe responsibility, but Mr. Johnson did so anyway. He was of a "judging" disposition which was consonant with his vocation for he was also a judge—and woe to the miscreants who came his way!

The spinster authoress seized particularly on the purported letters between the two ladies, which had been entirely in jest and joke, to injure their reputations. But the true story is all to Lady Susan's credit. Her only objective had been to raise the depressed spirits of her friend—trapped in an oppressive domestic arrangement—by treating the events of their lives in comical terms. The two friends understood this confidential language; their declarations, while in that mode, bore no resemblance to their true sentiments! But how delighted some authors are to misrepresent and readers to believe them.

Lady Susan had first learned of her banishment from the Johnsons' Edward Street house in October when she had stopped there on her way from Langford to Churchill. Mrs. Johnson had broached the subject immediately:

"You didn't receive my letter?"

"Letter?"

"Mr. Johnson forbids my seeing you."

"That's preposterous!" Susan laughed. "By what means 'forbids'?"

"He threatens the severest punishment imaginable—sending me back to Connecticut."

"To be tarred-and-feathered?" Susan jested, still not quite crediting this edict.

"The dangers I'd prefer not to ascertain; Mr. Johnson claims to have important business at Hartford and threatens to settle there if our connection is not entirely severed."

"But for what possible reason or pretext?"

The pretext, it turned out, was some absurd tittle-tattle regarding Lady Susan's stay at Langford. Such had come to Mr. Johnson's attention and he had reacted with this Draconic prohibition. So, a judge treats uncorroborated hearsay!

But by November the friends had decided that the ban must only relate to meeting within the Edward Street house itself.

A return to town, however exasperating the original impetus (in this case Frederica's flight), was always a tonic to Lady Susan's spirits. Barred from home she instead met her friend at the stately Adams Arcade, there recounting Frederica's recent misadventure with her usual good humour which, in my view, is the mark of an excellent disposition.

"I had no notion of Frederica's being so contrary!" she concluded. "She seemed all Vernon milkiness—but it confirms the rightness of my plan: Did Sir James call?"

"Several times."

"Excellent!"

"I followed your instructions, scolding him roundly for making love to Maria Manwaring—he protested that it had only been in joke! We both laughed heartily at her disappointment and, in short, were very agreeable. You are right: He's wonderfully silly."

Despite this phrasing I cannot imagine that either lady considered Sir James in any way "silly." I understand this to have been an affectionate term the two friends used, between themselves, for a man whom they enormously liked and respected, as indicated by their use also of the adverb "wonderfully." The spinster authoress clearly sought to use the word in another way, to deprecate Sir James. To feel themselves "higher" there are persons who make a virtual vocation of putting others "lower"—and this was true of the spinster authoress for whom even His Highness the Prince Regent was a figure to be mocked and deprecated. The affectionate epithet represented the sort of facetious language the two friends delighted in using with each other. I think we have all had such conversations; we would never want them set down, even in private manuscript.

"Perhaps one day I will see Frederica's escapade as having advanced my plan," Susan said. "But we can't let Sir James forget with whom he's in love—a man so rich and silly will not remain single long." (Again, the word is used here as a term of affection I am quite certain.)

"Sir James is so far from having forgotten the Vernons I'm sure he would marry either of you at the drop of a hat!"

"Thank you, my dear!" Alicia's acknowledgement of her continuing power pleased her.

Across the arcade's interior courtyard, or arcade-yard, a gentleman noticed the ladies and began to cross towards them, with his footman following.

"I must now return to Churchill," Lady Susan sighed. "But should Miss Summers refuse to take Frederica back I will need your help in finding another school. Under no circumstance will I have her at Churchill!"

"Very wise, my dear."

"What do you mean?"

"The nearness of their ages: hers and Reginald's."

The implication of this observation greatly irritated Susan; such fugitive, ill-conceived remarks often cloud relations between friends.

"How unkind."

"Forgive me!"

"Forgiven!" Lady Susan exclaimed, her sunny mood returned. "'The Fallacy of Youth!' Isn't it rather clear we, Women of Decision, hold the trumps!"

They both laughed, again united.

"Lady Susan? Lady Susan Vernon?"

The intruding voice was that of the gentleman who had crossed towards them.

"How dare you address me, Sir!"

The gentleman was taken aback.

"But…" he stammered, "Lady Susan—"

"Begone, Sir! Or I will arrange to have you whipped!"

The man turned on his heel and walked away, his footman scrambling to follow.

"Outrageous!" Alicia said. "You had never seen him before?"

"Oh, no, I know him well—I would never speak to a stranger that way."

Such was Lady Susan's delightful spirit, full of surprises, which her friends so savoured. Her actions, ostensibly puzzling, were nearly always justified. Perhaps, in this instance, this particular gentleman had no bad history or intention; it might seem harsh treatment for no worse infraction than greeting a distinguished lady in a public place. But if not he, surely others like him, at some point, had offended against their sex, perhaps often—so in general terms the rebuke was well justified.

"The Grand Affair of Education"

In Lady Susan's and Charles Vernon's first meeting with Miss Summers, that lady continued the pretence that her concern was Frederica's conduct rather than payment for her school's excessive fees. When Charles insisted on settling whatever fees were owed, Miss Summers refused, pending a decision on Frederica's continuance at the school—Lady Susan, however, was able to see through this tactic also.

Later, when Lady Susan mentioned her fatigued state to Charles, he reacted swiftly, urging her to return to Churchill; he would remain in town to pursue a more favourable outcome. Would Frederica be allowed to remain at school? Susan vibrated with concern for her daughter's future. Should Frederica not be allowed to remain at Miss Summers', where might she go? The ignominy of being "sent home" to Churchill must be avoided at all costs!

The next day, returned to Churchill, Lady Susan unburdened herself of these concerns as she walked with Reginald.

"You cannot know the emotion a mother feels when her child is—or could have been—in danger. We cannot regard our children coolly: Nature won't permit it. You perhaps see Frederica's actions as the dangerous egotism of a wilful child; I cannot."

"But you believe she's safe?"

"Physically—yes. But I'm frightened by what this reveals of an erratic nature. One loves one's child dearly, however selfishly she might behave. Can you comprehend that?"

"Yes—but I cannot help seeing in her behaviour a terrible irresponsibility which rather outrages me. Whilst I know that, as a mother, you must see everything she does with maternal softness—"

"Yes: I would never represent my daughter as worse than her actions show her to be."

Catherine Vernon was passing through the ground floor rooms with a letter for Lady Susan when she saw her and Reginald entering from the garden, Susan looking uncharacteristically fragile.

"Take a seat, rest," Reginald said as he helped Susan to the nearest sofa.

"Forgive me," Susan said. Always polite and considerate, Lady Susan felt constrained to apologize even for her faintness, which the heedless conduct of children has ever caused mothers.

"Susan, the afternoon coach brought this note," Catherine said, handing it to her. "Perhaps Charles has succeeded with Miss Summers."

Susan, her fingers quite trembling, broke the note's wax seal and read its first lines.

"It's as I feared...Miss Summers refuses to keep Frederica— she says she must think of her school's reputation—"

"Preposterous!" Reginald exclaimed. "I have never heard of her school!"

Not long thereafter the sound of horses and carriage echoed from the Churchill forecourt.

"Could that be them?" Reginald asked.

"What, Frederica? Here? Already?"

Lady Susan rose to see Charles and Frederica coming from the front hall in their traveling attire.

"Hullo, hullo. Well, here we are," Charles Vernon announced pertinently.

"Is this Frederica?" Catherine asked.

"Yes," Charles said. "Allow me to introduce our niece—charming girl—Miss Frederica Vernon."

"Welcome, Frederica! We have longed to know you…My brother, Reginald DeCourcy."

"Hullo," Reginald nodded. "Pleased to meet you." A certain coolness could be detected; he had already heard much in Frederica's disfavour.

Frederica was left facing her mother.

"Good afternoon, Frederica."

"Good afternoon, Mother."

Suddenly Frederica burst into tears and ran from the room. All looked startled except Lady Susan, who maintained an exemplary composure:

"It is as I had feared…Excuse me, I must go to my daughter."

Lady Susan—patient, graceful, compassionate—left to find her child.

"What was that?" Reginald asked. "Extraordinary."

"Poor Frederica," Catherine said, already her ally.

"Poor mother of Frederica!" Reginald replied.

"What?"

"The daughter is, I understand, a…troubled girl."

"I only saw fear."

The tension between brother and sister had grown like a black cloud from which, at any moment, lightning might strike. Wherever Lady Susan was concerned, opinions clashed—neither thought the other reasonable. This often happens when people disagree.

"Frederica hasn't had tea," Charles said. "It could be lack of nourishment."

Catherine left to have a second tea service prepared.

"Charming girl—though quiet," Charles said when he and Reginald were left alone. "Have always appreciated that. Gives one the chance to think."

Valuing Friendship Highly

Frederica's arrival posed another conundrum: Where was she to stay? Mrs. Cross already occupied the logical spot, the small room connected to Lady Susan's suite. The castle's South and East wings were still in disrepair, leaving the servants' wing the only practical alternative. The Brown Room there, though small, was actually quite pleasant, and Lady Susan considered it entirely adequate for Frederica's comfort, while recognizing that such decisions were properly the Vernons'.

Years later an aged Churchill retainer described to me the "ashen look on Mrs. Cross' face" as she and her small trunk were removed to the new location. (When I visited Churchill I was myself lodged in the Brown Room and am certain no slight or disrespect was intended.)

The worry over the rooms turned out to have been needless. Within the fortnight Mrs. Cross would depart Churchill. Lady Susan stood at the window of Churchill's great hall watching as Mrs. Cross' small trunk was carried to the carriage. One can imagine the poignancy of her feelings as her friend and confidante departed. Charles Vernon joined her there as the carriage pulled off.

"Poor Mrs. Cross has been obliged to accept a paying position in Buckinghamshire," Lady Susan lamented. "As there was an element of friendship involved I realized that the paying of wages would be offensive to us both."

"You value friendship highly," Charles remarked.

"Yes. I hope I was of some help to her."

A Preposterous Situation —
Entirely of Our Own Making

Frederica's arrival did not curtail Lady Susan's and Reginald's daily walks, it made them even more welcome: In the open air they could comment on matters of mutual concern out of earshot of those whose views did not accord with their own.

"One loves one's family," Reginald remarked, "but listening to someone's constant complaints and petty criticisms grows wearisome..."

"I agree entirely," Lady Susan said with a smile. "Life is a gift the Lord has given us—it is incumbent upon us to find the delight in it, not just the inconveniences. But I am grateful to your sister for her hospitality."

"Yes—perhaps it is rather me who is petty to complain of it."

"Not at all. You are highly observant; I admire such perceptivity—not to mention perspicacity."

Such distinctions and verbal niceties would perhaps have gone over Reginald's head as, in candour, they do mine. But was such language, verging on the pretentious, truly Lady Susan's or rather invented by the spinster authoress who, as will be shown, was no stranger to pretension and presumption?*

Reginald nevertheless took the remark as a compliment, though avoiding any direct acknowledgement of the flattery as any gentleman should.

The handsome couple was then approaching the side of the castle where Frederica and Lady Susan were lodged.

"Where is Frederica now?" Reginald asked.

"In our rooms, practising the pianoforte."

"She practises quietly."

They both listened for the notes—but heard none. Susan glanced up and back quickly.

"Don't look—Frederica is watching us."

"'Watching us'?"

"Yes, at the window—don't look."

"How odd...to be spied upon."

"That's the parent's lot! We bring these delightful creatures into the world—eagerly, happily—and then before long they are spying upon and judging us, rarely favourably. Having children is our fondest wish but, in doing so, we breed our acutest critics. It is a preposterous situation—but entirely of our own making."

Susan spoke not in exasperation but with a charming laugh.

"I marvel at your good humour."

"What alternative have we? It's the way of the world. We must accept it with a smile." Whereupon Lady Susan showed

---

* The language does not appear in the authoress' false "True Account" included as an appendix to this volume. However it was cited in her pre-epistolary version of that narrative. I make no representation as to its authenticity.

Reginald the smile that had caused half of London—at least the male half—to fall in love with her. "Of course when the little ones are very small there's a kind of sweetness which partially compensates for the dreadfulness which comes after..."

"You worry for Frederica's future?"

"I worry for her present"—she said cheerfully—"acknowledging that the responsibility for securing her future rests with me..."

Reginald admired Lady Susan's capacity for treating even distressing or discouraging subjects, such as the disloyalty of younger generations, with a thoughtful lightness. It was, in his view, delightful.

Less delightful were the strategies the female DeCourcys used to undermine her, such as so warmly and quickly embracing her disobedient, recalcitrant daughter.* Reginald was the particular target of his sister's remarks. They were sitting in the Gold Room, Catherine occupied with her needlework, he reading *The Gentleman's Magazine,* when she commented, "Frederica is quite prettier than I ever imagined."

"Pretty?" Reginald replied. "You think so?"

"Yes. You don't?"

"No... Quite the grey mouse, isn't she? In any case, beauty matters little: It is vivacity and lively conversation that one looks for, even from the young."

"You don't recognize what that is?"

"Yes: a lack of vivacity and conversation."

"No, Frederica's afraid of her mother."

Reginald smiled. "Impossible!"

---

* I later grew to admire Frederica but at this stage her behaviour was without question disloyal as the reader will soon learn.

"What?"

"The cunning of the girl—"

"Cunning?"

"Representing herself the victim—"

"Her mother says that?"

"No—like most mothers Lady Susan has the tendency to indulge her child."

"I have seen no such tendency!"

"Perhaps your ideas of what's indulgent, and what's not, are not entirely typical."

"What do you mean?"

A carriage and horses could be heard entering the forecourt, but the distraction was not sufficient to rescue Reginald from the disastrous path he had begun down: that of questioning, even to the minutest degree, how a mother raises her child.

"Any mother," he said, retreating, "having undergone the rigours of childbirth, has the right to her own view of child-rearing."

"What's wrong with my view of child-rearing?"

"Nothing *wrong*..."

"But not 'typical'?"

"Well, you'll admit you let them run a little wild. Lady Susan, raised at a stricter time, has different views—"

Just then there could be heard a commotion in the front hall and the sound of an unfamiliar, piercing male voice. Catherine rose as a distraught Frederica burst in, out of breath.

"Oh, I'm sorry! Excuse me—" Embarrassed to find Reginald, she halted. "I beg your pardon!"

"What is it, my dear?" Catherine asked.

"He's here! He's come! Sir James is here!"

Neither brother nor sister knew of whom she spoke; both were surprised at the extent of her discomposure.

"Excuse me. I'm sorry—" Frederica said, leaving to flee up the stairs.

"Frederica! Miss Vernon!" Sir James Martin called after her. Then, entering the room with Lady Susan, he continued: "So sorry to come like this. I suppose you didn't expect me."

Lady Susan did not reply, proceeding coolly to the introductions:

"Catherine, let me introduce Sir James Martin. Sir James, my sister-in-law, Mrs. Catherine Vernon, and her brother, Mr. Reginald DeCourcy."

"Hullo," Sir James said with a wide smile.

"How do you do?" they replied.

Sir James, surprised by the question, took some time to consider it. A broad smile passed over his face. "Excellent!" he replied, delighted by their interest. "Truly very well, thank you…

"Excuse my hurry in coming," he continued, "the lack of notice beforehand, et cetera. Truth is, I forgot to write—then it was too late. Now I'm here. Took the liberty of a relation, hoping to be one soon," Sir James nodded in the direction Frederica had gone. The others remained mute, as if bewildered. The spinster authoress describes Sir James as punctuating each phrase with a laugh; this is a common, low tactic of disparagement. The purpose: to make an honourable gentleman seem a "laughing fool."

"I must say, you looked surprised," Sir James said, turning to Lady Susan. "You were astonished to see me. No? Not? Well, that's how it looked."

"Yes, I was astonished—and still am."

Sir James then addressed Reginald: "An impressive establishment you have here, Sir. Congratulations. Immaculate."

"Mr. DeCourcy is Mrs. Vernon's brother—" Susan explained.

"Very good!"

"It is her husband, Mr. Vernon, who has Churchill."

"Churchill? That's how you say it? All-together that way?"
Sir James then pronounced the word very quickly, all-together:
"*Churchill*...That explains a great deal. I had heard 'church'
and 'hill'—but I couldn't find either...All I saw was this big
house." He laughed* again, then addressed Reginald.

"Fine name: 'Churchill.' Marlborough,** right? The general. He showed the French!" Sir James laughed. "You must be
very proud."

"No connection," Reginald said.

"But I believe I have heard it spoken of." Sir James turned
to Susan: "I think you mentioned it— '*Churchill*'—yes, I believe
you did but what I heard was '*church*' and '*hill*.' Couldn't find
them for the life of me!" Sir James smiled—his high spirits and
good humour should have been contagious, but good humour
and high spirits were alien to the DeCourcys; their demeanour
was wholly chilly.

"Mr. DeCourcy," Lady Susan began, "would you be so
kind as to take Sir James to see Mr. Vernon? Sir James, I believe

---

* Regarding the frequent mention of Sir James' laughter I must repeat that
this all, or mostly, derives from the anonymous authoress who sought,
for her own and the DeCourcys' purposes, to denigrate him as a foolish
simpleton.

** John Churchill, 1st Duke of Marlborough (1650–1722), led victorious
campaigns against Louis XIV's French forces; later, a victim of Whig
slander.

you will find Mr. Charles Vernon well versed in the advanced agricultural methods in which you've taken such an interest."

"Oh, yes!" Sir James said. "Advanced agricultural methods— very much so. Collins, who supervises Martindale for me, speaks of them often. The landowner of the present day must know all sorts of things—that's our role. 'Hullo, Collins'—I say—'what advanced methods have we today?' Excellent!"

The others regarded Sir James with surprise, perhaps due to his unusual enthusiasm for innovative agricultural techniques, a subject upon which our landed aristocracy has traditionally been recalcitrant.

A Family Matter

Perhaps this is a convenient juncture for me to touch on my own connection to the story. Sir James Martin was my uncle, my mother's beloved elder brother. Our Uncle James—or "Uncle Sir James" as we sometimes called him (or "Sir Uncle James," as Frederic, my younger brother, had it)—was a man who, under whatever titular form, brought only joy and good feeling into the world. Part was the affirmative pleasure of knowing someone always enthusiastic, always kind, always interested and pleased; part was the negative, nasty pleasure others found in mocking and ridiculing a man who would not conform to their icy mores. Prime among this latter group would, of course, be the DeCourcys—and that anonymous authoress who made herself their acolyte. The derision so unfairly directed at my uncle came largely from this quarter. In one of the supposed "letters" (no. 9) which the spinster lady concocted for her slanderous account, she has Mrs. Johnson write Lady Susan that Sir James "laughed heartily" and was "as silly as ever." This phrasing suggests a continuum of being "silly"—"silly as ever"—as if both women considered Sir

James silly long before this meeting with the assumption that he would continue being silly afterward, not that there was just one particular moment when he was silly.

(Might we not acknowledge that all of us might be considered "silly," if only for brief periods? Who is so proud as to say, "I have never, even for a moment, been silly?" What utter nonsense, what arrogant rot. Though, on reflection, it is true that the DeCourcys might well have been just that arrogant. "I have never been silly"—yes, it is possible to imagine Reginald DeCourcy, Lady DeCourcy, or Catherine née DeCourcy Vernon saying or thinking just that, despite the utter absurdity of such a prideful boast.

In letter number 20, perhaps the crucial one, the spinster authoress has Catherine Vernon write that "Sir James talked a great deal," that he mixed "more frequent laughter with his discourse than the subject required," "said many things over & over again," "told Lady Susan three times," and "concluded by wishing, with a laugh..." The strategy of deprecation employed here is familiar to those who have studied the subject: "Constant repetition" is a characteristic of imbeciles, as is "frequent and inappropriate laughter." A fine picture she paints of a good and honourable man!

Then, revealing her scandalous malice, she has him termed a "fool" (letter no. 23), a "Rattle" (no. 20), and "no Solomon" (no. 22)—this reference being to the wise king in the Bible. How fair can it be to compare anyone of recent times with such a Biblical wise man?

The excess of propriety and formality in our day has sadly deprived our language of many of the fertile and resonant words which the Englishman of prior centuries had at his disposal. "Argufy" is one such; the dictionary defines it as "to argue or quarrel, typically about something trivial." Certainly we have all seen occasions where innocuous subjects are "argufied"; an excess of drink is often involved, though, in my opinion, an excess of coffee or tea can lead to argufication also. The analogous "speechify" one still hears, though it cannot be considered elegant. Most useful, though less known, is the venerable "despisefy." Despisefy, or despisefying, is when a mass of people is led to despise someone or something for little or no reason.*

This is precisely what was done to my uncle. He was a good man, certainly nothing justified the deprecation to which he was subject, but by widely circulating the notion that he was silly and ridiculous he was left discredited in the circles influenced by the DeCourcy clique. Then, these circles influenced other circles. Soon, everyone was guffawing about Sir James Martin!** Yet if any of this great mass of gawfers had been pressed to explain why they were laughing, they would have been unable to do so. Sir James had been "despisefied."

★ ★ ★ ★ ★ ★

But what of Frederica? The question, posed earlier in our account, here becomes especially pertinent. After Frederica's hurried departure from the Gold Room, a lively concern for

---

* A sharp distinction should be maintained between "despised," as was the radical John Wilkes, and "despisefied," as was my uncle. Wilkes was either admired or despised for true reasons, not just from the haughty contempt of an aristocratic clique. Wilkes' distant relative John Wilkes Booth, assassin of the American President, Abraham Lincoln, was also truly despised, for good reason, not merely despisefied.

** "Guffaw" was already in use in those times; the term, dating from the Sixteenth Century, derives from the Scottish "gawf," onomatopoeia for a boisterous or vulgar laugh.

her daughter's well-being and perhaps even sanity pressed heavily upon Lady Susan's heart. As for any mother, her greatest concern was always the welfare of her child.

While Reginald DeCourcy and Sir James Martin left the house to search out Mr. Vernon, Lady Susan went to look for Frederica, going first to their rooms.

"Frederica? Darling?" she called softly. "Where are you?"

The passage between their rooms was dark, as was Frederica's room itself, all the curtains closely drawn. Lady Susan stepped carefully to avoid stumbling while she allowed her eyes to adjust to the gloom.

"Are you hiding here, my sweet?...Don't be afraid—let me hear from you...Oh, there you are! Were you asleep?"

"No, Mother."

"Well, what then? Were you hiding from me?...Please explain."

Once again nearly faint with worry for her daughter's welfare, Lady Susan sat on the small chair next to the bed where Frederica lay, her face buried in her pillow.

"You're a strange girl. What were you up to back there? Rushing out before Sir James entered the room..."

"I couldn't bear to see him."

" '*Couldn't bear*'? What an ungenerous manner of speech!"

Frederica neither moved nor responded; she continued lying face down on her bed, practically motionless.

I challenge anyone to argue that such behaviour or posture was either polite or respectful, or that in tolerating or indulging such behaviour Lady Susan was not putting at risk the character of her child as, unfortunately, so many mothers do; the consequences are never favourable.

"Frederica dear, Sir James Martin is a kind-hearted young

man whose only offence seems to be wanting to provide you a life of comfort."

She waited for a response; there was none.

"Have you nothing to say?"

Frederica shook her head.

"Dearest, our present comfortable state is of the most precarious sort. We don't live—we visit. We are entirely at the mercy of our friends and relations, as we discovered so painfully at Langford. Here you seem to have won your aunt's affection; I think I served you well there, for I believe she would do anything to spite me. But such a dynamic cannot continue forever."

Frederica sat up on her bed. "But, Mama—"

"'But, Mama'? I will not always be here for you to contradict me. If the life of comfort such as Sir James offers you is not to your taste, what will you do? How will you live?"

"I could...teach."

"Teach! Had you been more in school you would not consider such a thing!"

It is true that in the last century the teaching vocation was of little esteem and less profit, a state of affairs which Frederica, rarely in school, might not have known; fortunately in our own day these deficiencies have been corrected.

"Answer this," Lady Susan finally asked. "When our Lord wrote His Commandments, which one did He consider so important He put it in the fourth position?"

"The fourth position?"

"Yes, the Fourth Commandment."

"I know the Commandments—but not their order."

"See: This is what comes of an irregular education! The Fourth Commandment..."

Frederica began hesitantly: "'Thou shalt not...'?"

"It's not a 'Shalt not.' It's a 'Shalt.' "

" 'Thou shalt'?"

"Had I not myself been present I would wonder if I were even your mother!"

Susan gave her daughter a compassionate look despite her surly behaviour; on the subject of religion Frederica's education had been as defective as in every other respect. Lady Susan realized she would have to supply the information which her daughter's education had neglected. She cited the commandment which had eluded Frederica: "Honour—Thy—Father—And—Mother."

"I'm sorry, have I done anything that has dishonoured you or Father?"

"To 'honour' means, among other things, to listen with respect to a parent's sincere counsel."

"I do listen with respect, Mother. It's just that—"

"If you will not pay attention to me, then perhaps you will to a larger imperative: the Law of the Universe. An offer as splendid as Sir James' is not likely to come again. He has offered you the one thing of value he has to give—his income. I fear, and reproach myself, for having shielded you for far too long: Had I let you starve a little bit more, you would resist much less."

"But Mama, I was often hungry at school—"

"Evidently not hungry enough! In any case the starvation of the schoolhouse is nothing like that of the destitute. Is that what you want?"

"No...I can see that Sir James is a kind man and if it were not a matter of marriage I could like him. But marriage is for one's whole life—"

"Not in my experience. Meanwhile I must ask you not to speak to your aunt or uncle about this matter—or seek their interference in any way. I insist—promise...Remember the commandment."

"Yes, Mother."

★ ★ ★ ★ ★

The next day, walking with Catherine Vernon, Lady Susan sought to air her concerns about Sir James' reception at Churchill, not yet realizing to what degree her sister-in-law's ill-will made her impervious to the conciliating effect of such confidences.

"Sir James' arrival, and its suddenness, requires some explanation," Lady Susan began. "You were not too surprised, I hope?"

"It was unexpected—"

"Yes; certainly. To me, as much as anyone. I'm afraid Sir James' best qualities are not immediately apparent...Certainly, he's no Solomon★—"

"Solomon?"

"The wise king in the Bible...the one who had the idea of dividing the infant disputed by two mothers in half, or in two—I can't recall the exact wording."

"Oh, yes, of course."

"So, Sir James is no Solomon—but how many suitors of great wisdom is a young woman likely to find today?"

"I don't know—"

"None! And I must confess that at times I wonder if such a quality is even desirable in a husband..."

Catherine Vernon might have felt the jab of this remark: Although I grew to respect Charles Vernon's understanding as

---

★ Biblical king, known for his wisdom (1 Kings 3:16–28).

well as discernment, Catherine must have known that many in her circle questioned both. Among the habitually malicious, kindness and gentility are often mistaken for simple-mindedness.

"When you have the happiness of bestowing your sweet Emily on a man who's alike unexceptionable in his connections and character you may know how I feel. Though Emily will not, thank Heaven, depend upon a fortunate establishment for her survival!"

They walked in silence for a few paces before Catherine spoke.

"But...Sir James, isn't he...?"

"I know...He seems timid, and therefore awkward, occasionally saying things better left unsaid—in fact, a bit of a 'Rattle.'"

"Yes."

"Yet I think you'll find that his good qualities—and advantageous circumstances—outweigh whatever deficiencies an ungenerous or rancourous person might accentuate..."

Susan then asked—in the direct, candid manner that so disconcerted the retrogent*—if she might count on her and Mr. Vernon's blessing.

"Excuse me?"

"Might I count on your and Mr. Vernon's blessing for this connection, so important for Frederica's future happiness?"

"Well—I..." Catherine equivocated. "I think Charles should know him first."

---

* *Retrogent,* from the Latin, refers to those who interpret positive facts and qualities as their opposite, who find the dark lining within every silver cloud; sadly, a common trait in our country though the word itself is now rare.

The Very Unfair "Green Peas" Affair

The next incident of my uncle's stay at Churchill I must recount with a certain caution as it has been so unfairly used to despisefy him. A full explanation of the circumstances should, however, stand him acquitted of the reprehensible slanders to which he has been subject.

That green peas have not always been part of our English diet is not universally known. The green pea was introduced to the French court from Italy in the latter half of the Sixteenth Century. Its first appearance was met with some amazement, as well it might have been; the green pea is a peculiar legume, nearly perfectly round, something which occurs rarely in nature.* After the green peas' royal introduction it still took decades for peas-consumption to become habitual in even the highest French circles: At the century's end both Françoise d'Aubigné, the Marquise de Maintenon, second wife of King Louis XIV ("le Grand," or "the Great"), and Marie de Rabutin-Chantal, marquise de Sévigné, could still describe green peas as "a fashion, a fury."

---

* Excluding pearls and some berries.

Given these circumstances it should not be considered surprising that some decades later a representative of our ancient landed aristocracy, which had for eight centuries successfully resisted all invasion or infiltration from that direction, might not have been familiar with this French vogue.

Perhaps most importantly my uncle visited Churchill in an awkward role, that of *suitor.* He was a young man in love; his fervent, feverish hope to win Frederica Vernon's hand and affections was not faring well. Maybe it would be too much to say that Sir James was *desperate* because such theatricality was foreign to his nature. But he must have been disconcerted by his predicament.

As regards Frederica, Sir James faced not just coldness—as nearly all men courting young women must (usually further inflaming the romantic impulse)—but a sort of terror; and, for a mild man such as my uncle, that was a true barrier. He would have been appalled to think he was causing Frederica distress.

Jealousy was also a factor. At the fateful dinner Catherine Vernon insidiously arranged the seating so that Frederica was placed next to Reginald DeCourcy, with Sir James at the opposite extremity. Reginald, even Sir James could see, had Frederica's attentive regard. For a young man in love, this was deeply wounding; doubly so that in comparing himself with Reginald, as rivals in love will do (rivals as perceived by Sir James, not Reginald), he came up short. The younger man— whom he could recognize as having the advantage over him in terms of looks, position, et cetera—intimidated him. Made nervous, Sir James probably acted more "silly" than he might have otherwise. I would argue, quite passionately, that to act "silly" on occasion does not make one a "silly man."

A final, crucial factor might seem anomalous: our national

fascination, or perhaps obsession, with balls, even very small ones. Sir James had been mad for them since his time at Westminster. Like many of our greatest leaders, during his school years Sir James was far keener on moving balls on a playing field than studying globes or Greek and Latin conjugations. Each term a number of boys was "sent down" from school for neglecting their studies. Sir James was the first student to be "sent up" from Westminster (though this factum was later disputed, with some claiming that it was so phrased "in joke"; in any case Sir James was rusticated* from school for allowing his spherical preoccupation to take precedent over everything else).

Service at dinner that evening was strangely disordered. A helping of green peas was deposited on Sir James' entirely bare plate; the Vernons' Staffordshire creamware was exceptionally smooth; the peas—very round, very green, and perhaps under-cooked—rolled around gaily.

"How jolly," Sir James said, taking his knife and knocking the peas about a bit, laughing as he did so. "Tiny green balls!"

Sir James' high spirits, entirely understandable in the circumstances, attracted the notice of the others at table, which included several persons who did not wish him well. (Lady Susan was absent; feeling indisposed she had requested dinner in her room.)

"Perhaps they are under-cooked," Catherine said, with a concerned look.

"Nonsense, they're perfect," Charles Vernon replied.

---

* From the Latin verb *rusticārī*, meaning to live or stay in the country or to practise farming. Since the early Eighteenth Century "rusticate" came also to refer to students being "sent down," or "up," from a leading university or public school. *Rustic* is derived from the adjective *rūsticus*.

Sir James savored a forkful.

"Mmm, yes, good-tasting—quite sweet...What are they called?"

For quite a few moments there was no reply until Reginald finally answered, "Peas."

"Oh, yes! No, I knew that! Of course, I recall now...I must get Collins to cultivate them at Martindale. Novelty vegetable—could make quite a packet."

He took another taste. "Yes, distinctly sweet."

I suppose what the DeCourcys found so very mirthful in this episode was the idea that, long after green peas had become a familiar legume in the rarefied circles to which they were accustomed, Sir James did not know what they were, or what they were called. I would submit that the incident showed nothing of the kind. Sir James himself stated, "I knew that—I recall now," showing that it had just slipped his mind. Finally, one might ask, is this matter of peas really of such astounding importance? The DeCourcys, for their own interested motives, liked to pretend that it was. I would submit that it was not.

When after dinner the gentlemen joined the ladies in the Gold Room, Charles took Catherine aside: "I am enjoying Sir James' visit. His conversation is lively, he brings a new angle to things. What would you think if I took him to see the Fredericksville farm? He's mentioned his interest in the new agricultural methods..."

"Yes," Catherine replied with her usual deceptive smile. What was she thinking? One can only be certain: nothing good or kind.

There was, in fact, nothing ridiculous about Sir James' comments regarding peas. They had been under-cooked, were very green, and rolled remarkably well on the exceptionally smooth Staffordshire creamware; my uncle just happened to comment candidly upon them. And yet this "incident" has repeatedly been used to defame him.

* * * * *

But what of Frederica? At this point Frederica's actions and aspirations do bear close examination. What was her role, how intentional or inadvertent? That evening in the Gold Room after dinner she kept a watchful regard upon both young men: Sir James, who walked along the circumference of the room examining the paintings and mirrors, and Reginald, who was just then putting aside a volume of verse he had been reading. Frederica asked if she might look at it.

"Oh, yes. Please do."

"Just for a moment…" She picked it up to glance at it in a tentative manner.

"Oh, no, I'm finished—it's yours to read."

"Oh, thank you!"

Her disproportionate enthusiasm and gratitude disconcerted and, to a degree, disgusted him; the girl did seem as dull and pathetic as he had been led to believe. He felt obliged to explain: "I don't want to leave you under a false sense of obligation—I took the book from Mr. Vernon's library, so it is him you should thank."

"Oh, no, no need for that!" Charles said, re-entering the room. "Delighted to have these volumes exercised, taken out for a trot, or canter. That's what we have books for—to be read. Takes the burden off me for not attending to them as much as I should have. In fact," he said, addressing Frederica, "I believe that many of these books are from your late father's library, which I bought at auction to keep them within the fam—" Charles stopped abruptly, fearful that recalling the sad events surrounding her late father's ruin might wound Frederica. "Oh. Please excuse me—"

"Not at all, Uncle. I am very glad you should have them as I am sure that my father would have also."

"Thank you. Please do read them all—I mean, all those you would like to read..." With a polite nod Charles excused himself.

Sir James, having finished his examination of the room's decorations, rejoined the others.

"I admire the paintings," he said, "but the mirrors less so. Except, in the corner of that far mirror, I spotted a young woman who was rather pretty."

"That must have been Frederica."

Sir James thought a moment.

"I think you are right! Her reflection, no? That must be it. Thank you, Sir."

Another of my uncle's attractive qualities was that, when corrected, he did not argue or explain, he was merely grateful, which human nature normally resists, however illogically. We should always be grateful to learn what we do not know, or have others aid our understanding. We *should* be grateful, but among those I know only my uncle truly was.

Finally he turned to Frederica with a broad smile. "I must say, Frederica, I admired your reflection."

★ ★ ★ ★ ★ ★

How did Sir James Martin become my uncle? I believe I have written that my mother, Juliana Martin, was his younger sister. But it was only after she married my father, Giancarlo (later Jean-Charles) Colonna de Cesari-Rocca, a hero of the

Corsican fight for independence and a member of General Paoli's staff who followed him into London exile, that I was born and Sir James became my uncle—a role which was especially important after my father returned to the Mediterranean with General Paoli to resume that struggle.

My mother, Juliana Martin-Colonna de Cesari-Rocca—merely writing her name I am overcome with emotion, a profound and touching filial love—was Sir James' younger sister and favourite sibling. They were on the best of terms and strikingly similar in disposition: happy, kind, and entirely sanguine. During my childhood my mother was a great comfort to me, I was enormously relieved that she did not die prematurely as so many mothers did in those days. She had a profound understanding of the ways of boys small and not-so-small. It might surprise the reader but there was a time during my early years when I was the target of the apparent hostility of my form-mates, as well as members of the forms above and below my own. This hostility manifested itself in many ways: I was called ridiculous names, struck with fists, tripped up; my possessions were stolen or soiled; notes with unflattering words were attached to the back of my clothes where I could not see them but everyone else could. Ha, ha, ha. Or perhaps, more precisely: gawf, gawf, gawf.

The situation, this state of affairs, initially distressed me. I was terrified of going to school and, had I tear ducts, would have cried. Then one afternoon at tea time my mother revealed to me what it was all about: The other boys were intensely jealous of me. Apparently I had remarkable qualities and attributes (I had not known this) which made others envious. Having this information changed my perspective entirely: I had thought I was at the bottom of the heap at school but, as it turned out, I was at the top, which provoked an understandable resentment from my fellows.

A jealous emotion seized them and demanded an outlet—which manifested itself as contumely towards me. Henceforth when I was struck or had a sign or object pinned to my clothes I would even smile to myself—for what was this but flattery? There is a trite expression, "Imitation is the sincerest form of flattery." No, not at all; it is not the sincerest. That would be mocking contempt and physical battery—a lesson I learned, rather painfully, over a number of years.

★ ★ ★ ★ ★ ★

The next morning at Churchill Frederica could be seen before the fire in the main hall seemingly enthralled by the volume of Cowper's★ poetry that she had borrowed the evening before. But was she really so enthralled by it? Was not Frederica the sort of shy girl who always carried a book so that she might hide in its pages to avoid any social encounter she feared might be awkward, which was almost all of them? (An unsociable tactic her mother found intolerable.)

That morning as she read, Frederica occasionally looked up and stared into the fire as if she truly comprehended Cowper's verse and was reflecting upon it—when, in fact, she could have been thinking about anything or nothing at all. As I find both poetry and verse largely incomprehensible—except, of course, for the works of the great Pope★★—it is difficult for me to imagine or describe what others see in them. But perhaps Frederica was sincere; she did discuss Cowper's verse, suggesting it meant something to her—as Reginald did also. This was perhaps a first indication that they might be suited one to

---

★ William Cowper (1731–1800), poet and hymnodist.
★★ Alexander Pope (1688–1744), incontestably the greatest of our poets.

another, though Reginald then considered her dull and plain. In any case it is perhaps not in man's nature to judge women at their true worth.

Lady Susan arose with her indisposition of the previous evening happily past. At Reginald's entreaty she joined him to walk in the Churchill gardens.

"This man, Sir James Martin," he asked, "do you know him well?"

"To a certain extent."

"Why, might I ask, is he here?"

"I believe Sir James explained that himself: He knew no one in the vicinity and wanted to avoid staying at the inn, which I can well understand."

"He is utterly ridiculous."

"Certainly, he's no Solomon, but—"

"Solomon?"

"The wise king from the Bible; I know he's not that. But any man, navigating the cascades of romantic courtship, and occasionally falling into those foaming waters, is not apt to appear at his best."

"What?"

"A simple word, Reginald: 'Comprehension.' I admire your cast of mind, but you might not be entirely sensible of the degree to which you intimidate others—particularly a young man over whom you have every advantage of position, looks, and character."

I had assumed this also; it is very easy for one to get into a situation in which one is seen in an unfavourable light. My former wife considered me boring while I thought her unkind. The question I would ask is whether her ill-opinion of me preceded or followed her conduct—was it provoking or justifying? Those who fall from virtue first cause injury, then cast blame.

To Lady Susan's explanation Reginald responded:

"Sir James Martin is a fool because of me?"

"Yes. Around you he seems very silly."

"He isn't silly around everyone?"

"No," she said.

"I believe he's given everyone the same impression."

"They have only seen him around you."

"But you deny Sir James' intentions towards you?"

"Towards me?"

"He's clearly besotted with you."

Susan laughed as if surprised and flattered:

"No, it's with Frederica he's smitten."

"That's not possible."

"Well, he has proposed to her."

"How could such a blockhead even be allowed to court your daughter? It's incomprehensible."

"This is the 'incomprehension' of the rich and easeful! You can afford to take the high ground and add another layer to your pride. If you realized the full extent of ridiculous manhood a young girl without fortune must humour you would be more generous to Sir James."

$$\star \ ^\star \ ^\star \ _\star \ ^\star \ _\star \ ^\star$$

Happy news came for Lady Susan later that week: Mrs. Alicia Johnson, her American friend, sent word that her coach would be stopping at Hurst & Wilford to change horses, allowing time for a brief visit and exchange of confidences. Lady Susan found her friend in distress.

"Mr. Johnson is relentless," Alicia said. "I will not be sent back to Connecticut!"

"I don't see why he believes that association with me would lower your reputation. But, a question: When you saw Sir James did he mention any plans to come to Churchill?"

"Heavens no! What folly! How did Mr. DeCourcy react?"

"I must say, I had some gratification there. At first Reginald observed Sir James with an attention not untinged with jealousy. But it was impossible to really torture him—for I had to finally reveal that his object was Frederica. Then he was all astonishment! Left to ourselves I had no great difficulty in convincing him I was justified—I don't remember the exact reasoning but it was all comfortably arranged." I will shortly comment on this account of their conversation, which I consider essentially false.

"Young DeCourcy is not stupid—and has a great deal to say," Lady Susan is represented as having said. "But I can't help but look with a certain contempt on the fancies of the heart so doubting the reasonableness of its emotions. I vastly prefer the generous spirit of a Manwaring, who, deeply convinced of one's merit, is satisfied that whatever one does is right."

"I know that no one really deserves you, my dear, but young DeCourcy might be worth having."

This account I am certain neither presents the friends' conversation accurately, nor reflects Lady Susan's true perspective. The principal source was the spinster authoress' account, which she has, as usual, bent in their disfavour. "Dreadful nonsense!" Mrs. Johnson pronounced when I asked about it in later years. The portrayal of my aunt and her friend as cynical, self-interested women, grasping after fortunes, is a cruel travesty; it can quite easily be exposed as false, which I will shortly do.

* * * * *

The same afternoon that Lady Susan met Mrs. Johnson an interesting discussion took place at Churchill which malicious parties would later distort to viciously despisefy my uncle.

Frederica, Reginald, and Charles Vernon were reading in the Gold Room, each in a comfortable chair, when Matthew, the footman, brought in the recently arrived number of *The Gentleman's Magazine*. Sir James, entering shortly after, saw the magazine and picked it up.

"You enjoy *The Gentleman's Magazine,* Sir James?" Charles inquired affably.

"No, not really," Sir James replied, "but until they come out with *The Baronet's Quarterly* it will have to do."

Charles appreciated his jest. There was, of course, no *Baronet's Quarterly;* it was just an excellent joke on my uncle's part—his being a "baronet," not merely a "gentleman" such as Mr. Vernon, but there was no element of social presumption or snobbery in his remark, that being entirely foreign to his nature.

Sir James smiled and strolled in a casual manner towards the part of the room where Frederica sat reading. He swiveled towards her, then addressed her with his usual precise courtesy:

"Excuse me, Frederica," he said. "When I came down this morning I couldn't help but notice that you were reading a 'book.' Which 'book' was that?"

Frederica showed the book which she had been reading.

"This volume of Cowper's★ verse."

★ Pronounced "Cooper" except in Wales and by certain Cowper family descendants (the poet himself was childless). Though educated at Westminster, Cowper was not good at games, turning then to verse and hymnody.

"Cowper, the poet? He also writes verse? Most impressive."

"Yes," Reginald interjected, "he's versatile that way." (Verse-versatile was Reginald's version of a pun; the DeCourcys had little facility for wordplay.)

Sir James took a seat near Frederica.

"So, Frederica, you read both poetry and verse? In this I believe you take after your mother, who knows a great many things. Just yesterday she cited to me a story from the Bible about a very wise king. This reminded me of many such accounts one learns in childhood. Perhaps most significant in forming one's principles is that of the old prophet* who came down from the mount with tablets bearing the Twelve Commandments—which our Lord has taught us to obey without fail."

"The Twelve Commandments?" Reginald asked.

Sir James nodded affably in the affirmative.

"Excuse me," Charles interrupted in an apologetic tone, "I believe there were only Ten."

"Oh, really?" Sir James said. "Only Ten must be obeyed? Well, then…Which two to take off? Perhaps the one about the Sabbath," he said with a smile. "I prefer to hunt."

"Well…" Charles demurred.

"After that," Sir James continued, "it gets hard. Many of the 'Shalt nots'—don't murder, don't covet thy neighbour's house, or wife, one wouldn't do anyway, because They Are Wrong, whether the Lord allows us to take them off or not."

Sir James looked to Frederica to gauge her support; to see how favourably his observations had struck her. Her true sentiments, however, were difficult to detect.

---

* Moses, Old Testament prophet.

★ ★ ★ ★ ★
  ★   ★   ★

Sir James' "Twelve Commandments" discourse was obviously prank, quite good of its kind—but the humourless DeCourcys refused to let it be treated as such. Here they saw another opportunity to ridicule and injure my uncle and, through him, Lady Susan. Charles Vernon, however, was happy to admit that he found Sir James' talk amusing (the term used was "droll," derived from the French). He was chuckling when he remarked to Catherine, "I have to say, I enjoy Sir James' humour. Quite ingenious."

In any case the researches of Biblical scholars have since suggested that "twelve" could be closer to the mark when enumerating the commandments. Some have in fact identified fifteen commandments in the relevant text (Exodus 20:1–17), which would place Sir James' version closer to the correct one. This often happens: The individual who identifies a truth earlier than others is then bitterly mocked by those attached to erroneous convention.

To well understand my uncle a recourse to the wisdom of past eras is helpful. Physicians of earlier times saw man's nature in terms of the four "humours." While the "humours" are no longer part of medical orthodoxy, they still usefully describe behaviours and perspectives. The humours associated with "black bile" and "yellow bile"*—in the former case representing low or depressed spirits (melancholia), in the latter, an angry (choleric) disposition—would well characterise the DeCourcys and their spinster amanuensis. Angry individuals of a dark dis-

---

* From these we also get the adjective *bilious.*

position find a peculiar *soulagement*★ in attacking, deprecating, and ridiculing others, especially those of sanguine disposition such as my uncle. His happy disposition seemed to enrage them particularly.

A shameful prejudice against those with cheerful or generous sentiments has long marked our society—an assumption that those of a sunny outlook lack the understanding, intelligence, and gravity of those spilling bile. What a false and corrosive belief! In a similar way these yellow and black bile-fulls exaggerate into unpardonable "outrages" the small errors and missteps into which those of us engaged in the business of the world are occasionally led, despite our best efforts and entire goodwill. The unfairness and hypocrisy of this can make one extremely angry.

Most relevant is the conundrum posed by the ancients—I believe it was Demosthenes—who spoke of the "goblet" filled with liquid up to its midpoint: Is such a goblet "half full" or "half empty"? In answering this, those of a DeCourcy disposition would see emptiness and complain, "Why is this goblet not full?" Or even, "We have been cheated! The goblet is empty. Who has taken the rest?" I can almost hear their voices. They would see only the deficiency and protest it, bitterly and arrogantly.

My uncle's perspective was entirely otherwise. He would appreciate the smaller portion as appropriate, practical, even elegant. A goblet filled to its edge might well spill, causing harm, staining clothing or furnishings, as well as waste; at the minimum it would require careful sipping and could not be easily handed to a friend for sharing. A so-called "half-filled" goblet can, on the other hand, be moved about freely without

---

★ Solace, from the French.

spilling; it can be taken on a walk or journey. In fact, even the half that is seen as "empty" is not truly so; it is filled to the brim with healthful, life-giving "air." If one were trapped in an airless vault the "empty" half of the goblet could prove the difference between life and death. So, the goblet which others (the DeCourcys) would despisefy for its vacuity, Sir James would see and appreciate for its many, more significant advantages. His idealism was so pure, so elevated, as to be entirely beyond the comprehension of low and choleric souls such as the DeCourcys and their cynical scribe. In fact it eluded nearly everyone.

Sir James Martin Aids a Widow

Sir James' great hope was that Frederica would shortly become his bride, in which case Lady Susan would gain a new role—that of mother-in-law. (The recollection that at Langford it was the mother with whom he was first smitten seemed to have been put aside. Or had it?)

Sir James tried to think of the confidential steps that might be taken to relieve the narrowness of the admirable lady's finances. He decided to do so in the form of a loan for which repayment would not be needed or expected and, as it turned out, this was precisely the sort of financial arrangement Susan favoured also. Sir James, not wanting to intrude on her privacy, politely stood outside the partly open door to her rooms when discussing the loan's final details.

"It's so kind of you," Lady Susan said. (I can imagine her lovely voice—its sweet, rich tone—having become well acquainted with it in my childhood.★)

★ Even as eight-year-olds we were all a little in love with her. At that age sentiments are pure and idealistic, a warm glow suffusing one's consciousness. The disgusting thoughts and imaginings do not typically come for another five years or so.

"No, delighted...Honoured. My pleasure."

"Would you like me to sign a note?"

"No, no documents. No 'note' necessary. All in the family...or hoping to be soon."

"And the carriage?"

"Oh, yes, the carriage. Definitely. Certainly. My pleasure. Honoured."

That evening the Vernons held a dance in Churchill's great hall, with a band of five musicians brought in for the evening. The young curate from the Churchill parish and various neighbours attended, forming a not large but animated and congenial group. The high point, everyone thought, was the small orchestra's rousing rendition of the "Sir Roger de Coverly." Reginald was initially paired with Lady Susan and Frederica with Sir James. My uncle was in particularly high spirits that evening, greatly enjoying himself. Unfortunately, one person's high spirits can depress another's low spirits still further; that is what seems to have happened to Frederica. Even if one were to contend, as I would, that her aversion to Sir James' courtship was ill-founded and quite unfair, it was nevertheless passionately felt. After the dance Frederica was in even greater despair. That night she hardly slept.

* ★ * ★ * ★ *

The next day began a series of events and encounters which transformed the relations of all involved. Reginald DeCourcy, returning from his morning ride with Charles Vernon, was surprised to find Frederica already up, sitting by the fire in the great hall with her head buried in a volume (though, in fact, she was entirely aware of Reginald's arrival and had been lying in wait* for him).

"Oh, hullo. Good day," Reginald said, more affably than usual; pity for Frederica had come to outweigh the contempt.

"Would you know where I might find your mother?"

"I believe she's gone out."

"Gone out?"

Frederica did not reply. (The basis for this account are conversations I had with her many years later; from a personal knowledge of the other principals, as well as of Churchill Castle, I have added additional details of interest to the reader.)

Reginald, concerned at her apparent distress, came nearer while remaining standing. (Frederica's recollections could have been softened by being seen through the gauze of a retrospective romantic haze.)

"Are you all right?"

Frederica first nodded, then froze as if in fear or suffering from a debilitating stroke,** which would have been highly unusual at such a young age.

"What is it?"

Frederica could not reply.

"Tell me: What's wrong?"

Frederica looked too upset to speak, fearing that if she did venture a word she might burst into tears. Instead she said nothing, looking down at an indefinite spot on the floor.

---

* "Lying in wait," an expression that suggests a lurking posture preparatory to an ambuscade.
** An apoplectic seizure, derived from "Stroke of God's Hand" (Sixteenth Century).

"Please say," Reginald persisted.

"Sir, I... I do not know to whom I can apply."

"What is it? Please tell me."

"I am sorry, I shouldn't have said anything! It's that—that you're the only one Mother might listen to."

"Why would you say that?"

"She pays no one such regard as she does you, except Lord Manwaring."

"What do you mean, Manwaring?"

"No, I'm sorry!" Frederica said, panicking at her slip. "It's just that, of all people, I thought Mother would listen most to you."

"Let me understand this: It is that you find Sir James' presence and courtship of you unwelcome?" Reginald asked, finally sitting.

Frederica nodded.

"If his presence here disturbs you, it is to Charles or my sister to whom you should apply."

Frederica did not immediately reply.

"I—I promised Mother I would not."

"I don't understand. Why would you promise that?"

Frederica, realizing she had gone too far, became flustered. In a small voice she confessed: "She required it."

"What did she require?"

Frederica seemed again to freeze.

"What?... These silences are vexing."

"Mother forbade it."

"I don't understand."

"I promised not to speak to my aunt and uncle on this subject."

"For what possible reason?"

"It's wrong of me to speak now. If I were not at my wit's end I would not have—I can't marry Sir James!"

"To what do you object?"

Frederica was taken aback at the question; Reginald had seemed more critical of Sir James than anyone. I myself never understood Frederica's firm opposition to my uncle's suit. Perhaps there was an element of vanity: that she had not herself chosen the man being so emphatically proposed. A strong prejudice is so engendered against the suitor, whatever might be said in his favour. Nevertheless it remains painful for me to record how she answered Reginald that morning (which choice of words, I understand, she herself later greatly regretted):

"You must have noticed—he's very silly."

"But, besides that."

"Besides that?"

"Yes. I confess, the first impression I had of him was also . . . indifferent. But don't those knowledgeable of such matters consider Sir James a man of cheerful temperament, happy to devote a large income to a wife's comfort? And, as such, a good 'catch,' or 'match,' or whatever it is they say . . ."

The insufferable condescension and complacency of the DeCourcys! It rather outrages me. Of course, Reginald, heir to a substantial estate, firmly entailed, could afford to look down on such essential considerations. Not so easy for the rest of the world. Frederica, at least, was less presumptuous.

"I'd rather work for my bread!"

"But what could you do?"

"I could teach. I could—"

"Teach!" Reginald exclaimed. "You must have been very little in school to think that." This repeated slighting of the teaching profession, as if its low status, poor pay, and miserable practitioners should make it the sport of the arrogant, though less true in our own day, must, upon further reflection, be conceded to be essentially true.

"Tell me: How did this happen?" Reginald asked. "Your mother is a woman of excellent understanding, her concern for you great—though wise and clear-eyed. How could she be so mistaken as you suggest, if you truly despise Sir James?"

"I don't despise Sir James. I'm sure he is a kind man, and he has charm of a...sort. And certainly, he is likable, and I'm sure I could like him if he were a cousin, or a cousin's cousin, or a friend, or a friend's friend, or a connection, or step-something— I just don't want to marry him."

"Come." Reginald stood. "Tell me the particulars. If they are as you say I can't for the world imagine that your mother would remain deaf to your wishes."

Frederica was very wrong to have spoken to Reginald about this matter. Ungrateful for, and uncomprehending of, the efforts her mother was making on her behalf, Frederica closed her mind to a worthy young man while putting at risk her mother's and Reginald's cordial relations, so important to them both. Such behaviour is common among girls who have been indulged either too much or too little. I believe that later in life Frederica herself realized this. Reginald DeCourcy might have been handsome, both as a young man and in age, but Sir James was ever cheerful and amusing, whether intentionally or not, and over a long life those qualities come to have great value, in my opinion.

★ ★ ★ ★ ★ ★

An interview took place between Lady Susan and Reginald at this point of which we know only the posterior result and comment.

Afterwards Reginald joined Catherine in the Blue Room, where she was sorting through small trinkets she was preparing as Christmas presents. Though rich, Catherine was neither considerate nor generous; those who frequent such circles know that this seeming paradox is, in fact, quite ordinary.

"Catherine, I would like to thank you for this visit."

Reginald seemed somewhat agitated; there was a slight high colour or blush to his complexion.

"You are leaving?"

"Yes, I must."

"Why?"

"As you've said it's important that, at this season, one of us be with our parents."

"You've just decided this now?"

"Yes. But before going I must ask one thing: I'd be grateful if you could see justice is done Frederica. She's a sweet girl who deserves a better fate."

"I'm glad you now see her worth."

"Yes, my eyes have opened* to many things…"

---

* This impression of "eyes finally opening," alerting one to some truth or danger, occurs frequently—but it is almost entirely illusory. The implication is that, with eyes open, dangers will be discerned and so avoided, a notion which, though perhaps reassuring, is entirely false. Rarely does harm come to us when our eyes are closed, very often when they are open. In my own experience it is only when my eyes have been open that disasters have befallen me. Barring volcanoes, earthquakes, or house fires one is almost invariably safer when one's eyes are closed. But that is not the commonplace view, and Reginald DeCourcy was not the sort of man to plumb such matters deeply.

★ ★ ★ ★ ★
★ ★ ★

Not long after this conversation Frederica, in a visibly distressed state, descended the stairs and approached Catherine in the Gold Room.

"Aunt, I did something very wrong—"

"I'm sure not—"

"No, I did," Frederica insisted. "And now Mr. DeCourcy and my mother have quarreled: He is to leave and it is my fault! Mother will never forgive me—"

"Don't worry: If any of what you fear comes to pass, I'll happily intercede…"

Frederica retreated to her room, just missing her mother as she left hers. Lady Susan carried carefully in her hand a small, neatly-wrapped package.

"Good afternoon, Catherine. That cough of young Frederic's worries me—I have from London Dr. Preston's excellent lozenges. Might you take them for the dear boy?"

She handed Catherine the small packet, which carried the pleasingly printed motto, "Dr. Preston's Famous Lozenges for the Cough and Maladies of the Throat."

"Yes, thank you," Catherine said, a lack of sincere gratitude evident.

"Also, is it true that we will be losing Mr. DeCourcy today?"

"Yes, it seems that we will be."

"How remarkable! When he and I spoke, barely an hour ago, he made no mention of it…"

Susan examined Catherine's expression in search of an answer and believed she found it: "But, perhaps he then did not know himself. Young men are so impetuous in their resolutions—"

"I wouldn't say Reginald is impetuous—"

"Oh, yes, he is," Susan insisted lightly. "He's like other young men that way: Hasty in making resolutions and then just as quick to unmake them! I would be very surprised if he were not to change his mind and stay."

"He seemed quite decided."

"Well, we'll see..." Susan smiled. She started to leave, then stopped. "Some strangeness seems to be affecting Frederica too—I believe the girl's actually fallen in love, with your brother the object!"

Soon after this conversation, the same afternoon, Wilson, the butler, knocked at Reginald's door. Reginald, jacketless, opened it. The country aristocracy of that period conducted themselves with less formality than we do today, an occasionally rough manners-less-ness. The history of manners has been one of steady improvement and increased elegance.

"Sir, Lady Susan asked if she might have a word with you, if you would be so kind as to visit her in her dressing room." Wilson bowed and left. Reginald put on his jacket with an expression partly of longing, partly of dread. He slowly descended the stairs to the floor where Lady Susan's rooms were located and knocked on her door.

"Come in." Lady Susan's voice was weak, as if she had been in tears and was not fully recovered. She rose from her writing table as Reginald entered.

"I beg your pardon for calling you here, Sir, but I've just learned of your intention to leave today. Is that true?"

"Yes, it is."

"You may close the door," she said, her voice wavering. She took a seat and indicated for Reginald to do so also.

"I entreat you not, on my account, to shorten your visit by even an hour," she began. "I am perfectly aware that after what has passed between us it would ill-suit either of us to remain in the same house. But it is I, not you, who should go."

"No. Why?"

Lady Susan raised her hand.

"My visit has already been inconvenient for your family; for me to stay risks dividing a clan affectionately attached to one another. Where I go is of little consequence"—here the waver in her voice returned—"whereas your presence is important to all."

★ ★ ★ ★ ★ ★

In the Gold Room Catherine's concern was for Frederica's situation. Her hands busied with needlework; the great solace of such activities is how they allow the body to disconnect from the mind, normally a jealous tyrant. Reginald appeared in the room, standing in its midst, perfectly still.

"Reginald, Charles would like to speak with you before you go—"

"That won't be necessary."

"But...he wanted to speak with you about the hunt."

"What I mean is, I will not be leaving. I have decided to stay."

"Not go to Parklands?"

"No. There's been a terrible mistake." Reginald looked around as if to ensure that they were entirely alone. "Might I explain?"

"Yes, certainly, please do."

He took a seat.

"I am afraid I have acted with a discreditable impetuousness. In so doing, I have done Lady Susan an acute injustice. I was entirely mistaken and was on the point of leaving under a false impression. Frederica has misunderstood her mother; Lady Susan means the girl nothing but well—"

"Obliging her to marry Sir James Martin?"

"That has been misrepresented; the true problem is that Frederica will not make a friend of her mother—"

"Not make a friend of her?"

"Yes—it seems that during Mr. Vernon's prolonged illness Frederica's behaviour to her mother turned hostile. Such a posture—resenting a well-meaning parent—is apparently quite common among girls her age. I had no right to interfere— and Miss Vernon was mistaken in applying to me."

"But Lady Susan was obliging her to marry—"

"No, not at all. Frederica completely misunderstood her mother. A misunderstanding which has caused Lady Susan much concern; she has asked me to request the favour of an interview."

"An 'interview'? With me?"

"Yes. She is still quite discomposed and remains in her dressing room. Might you go to her?"

★ ★ ★ ★ ★ ★

"Come in."

The reply was pronounced in such a soft and fragile tone Catherine could scarcely make it out. She opened the door; Susan welcomed her with a poignant smile.

"My brother tells me that you wished to speak," Catherine said.

"Yes. Thank you for coming. Please have a seat."

When they had both settled at the set of chairs next to the fire, Susan began:

"Did I not express to you my fond hope that your brother would stay?"

"Yes. You certainly have an uncanny knack for divining the future where my brother is concerned."

"Please don't resent this intuition!" Susan exclaimed, her tone one of sad regret. "I shouldn't have hazarded any guess had it not, at that moment, occurred to me that his decision followed upon a heated discussion between us regarding Sir James' presence here. I know that Sir James seems 'under par'*—to some—his boyish manner and athletic interests, et cetera."

"Does that surprise you?"

"No. It is how Frederica went about making her opposition known—"

"I believe she feared you would be angry."

"I know. But, on the contrary, I applaud her good sense. It surprises and delights me."

"You were not aware of it?"

Susan considered the question. "No, I wasn't. Frederica rarely does herself justice. Her manner is shy, her habit of mind solitary. Perhaps her father's indulgent nature spoiled her to a degree; the severity I have had to show since has given her a strange fear of me. This *éloignement*** between us might have led Frederica to waylay Mr. DeCourcy and beg him to intercede on her behalf—"

"What other recourse had she?"

"My God, what must you think of me! Could you possibly believe I was aware how unhappy she was? For any mother our child's welfare is our first earthly promise and duty!"

"You didn't know she disliked Sir James?"

---

* "Under par"—the reference is to a bond that trades at less than its face or "par" value; note that this was not Lady Susan's view, but that of "some," such as those in the DeCourcy circle.

** *Éloignement,* French for estrangement, separation, distancement.

"I knew he was not the first man she would have chosen if left to her youthful, unformed judgement or, rather, ill-formed from reading the sort of novels that put terms such as 'Love' and the like in their titles. What harm such books do! But I was not persuaded her decision was firmly established."

Lady Susan paused, then leaned forward to take her sister-in-law into her confidence, a note of sadness again in her voice:

"There is something I have concealed: Frederica's applying to Mr. DeCourcy, and his instantly taking her part, hurt me greatly. His disposition is warm and when he came to expostulate with me his compassion was all alive for this ill-used girl! He thought me more to blame than I was, while I considered his interference less excusable than I now find it. When I understood his intention of leaving Churchill I resolved to have an explanation before it was too late. Now that I know the depth of Frederica's aversion to Sir James I reproach myself for having ever, though innocently, made her unhappy on that score. I shall instantly inform the poor man he must give up all hope of her!"

Even so many decades after these events it still makes my "blood boil" to read how my uncle was denigrated; thoroughly despisefied. It is no coincidence, I believe, that those who most deprecated Sir James were also those who calumniated Lady Susan and her charming American friend, Mrs. Johnson.

A ludicrous episode in the spinster authoress' chronicle recounts a supposed conversation (transposed, of course, into an exchange of letters) between Lady Susan and Mrs. Johnson, said to have taken place just after Lady Susan had regained London that December. It portrays Lady Susan as visiting Alicia at Edward Street (an impossibility since Mr. Johnson had banned her visits there).

"I call on you for congratulations, my dear! I am again myself—gay and triumphant—"

"Congratulations!" this account has Mrs. Johnson replying. "How wonderful—"

"But it's terrifying how close I came to destruction, only escaping at the last with a degree of insouciance that I must say surprised even me."

"Your friends have long known it, my dear—"

"What friends?" Susan joked; she was certainly aware of her many friends, but she enjoyed flattering Alicia's privileged position.

"I pride myself on being the only one, other than yourself, to know the extent of your brilliance."

"Thank you; but, there is no danger of Mr. Johnson surprising us?"

"I am happy to report that Mr. Johnson's gout has taken him to Bath where, if the waters are favourable, he'll be laid up many weeks."

The idea of Alicia Johnson's making such a statement is malicious invention; among other things Mr. Johnson detested Bath, considering Tunbridge Wells more respectable.

"It started with Frederica," Lady Susan began, "who, in the grip of a madness of some kind, entreated Reginald to intercede on her behalf—as if I were some unkind mother not wanting the best for my child! Reginald appeared at my rooms with an expression of the utmost solemnity to inform me of the impropriety of allowing Sir James Martin to court Frederica! I tried to joke him out of it but he refused to be. When I calmly required an explanation, begging to know by what he was impelled, by whom commissioned, to reprimand me he then told me—mixing in a few ill-timed compliments—that my daughter had acquainted him with some circumstances which gave him 'great uneasiness'—"

"Heavens, is he really so pompous?"

"The pomposity I assume; it's the disloyalty which outrages me. If he held me in true regard he would not believe such insinuations in my disfavour. A worthy lover should assume one has unanswerable motives for all one does!"

"Certainly—"

"Where was the resentment which true love requires against those who defame one's beloved? And she a child, a chit, without talent or education, whom he had been well taught to despise? I was calm for a time but the greatest forbearance may be overcome. He endeavoured—long endeavoured—to soften my resentment but at length left as deeply provoked as I was."

Obviously this account is gravely distorted; Lady Susan was devoted to her daughter as she stated on many occasions. Note how the clever (though not in a sense anyone could admire), unscrupulous authoress seeks to give an aura of "Truth" to her version by interweaving with it actual conversations.

"Scarcely an hour had gone by when I learned Reginald was leaving Churchill," Susan said (according to this version). "Something had to be done; condescension was necessary though I *abhor* it. I sent for Reginald; when he appeared the angry emotions which had marked his countenance were partly subdued. He seemed astonished at the summons, and looked as if half-wishing, half-fearing to be softened by what I might say—"

"With what admiration can I imagine the result!"

"The outcome justifies some portion of vanity, my dear, for it was no less favourable than immediate."

"You brilliant creature!"

"How delightful to watch the variations of his countenance while I convinced him of his error! To see the struggle between returning tenderness and the remains of doubt. There is something very agreeable in feelings so easily worked on. Yet this Reginald, whom a very few words from me softened at once into the utmost submission, and rendered more attached, more devoted than ever, would have left me in the first angry swelling of his proud heart without deigning to seek an explanation!"

"How outrageous—and yet, I'm afraid, characteristic of their sex..."

"Humbled as he now was, I found it hard to forgive him this eruption of pride. I wondered whether I ought to punish him by dismissing him at once—or by marrying and teasing him forever."

"Marry him! A man so easily influenced is to be treasured."

"As for Frederica, with her little rebellious heart and indelicate feelings, throwing herself on the protection of a young man she scarcely knew—her impudence and his credulity equally astound me. So now, my dear, I have many tasks: I must punish Frederica for her application to Reginald, and punish him for receiving it so favourably; torment my sister-in-law for the insolent triumph of her manner; and make myself serious amends for the humiliations I've been obliged to undergo."

"Where will you start?"

"I believe I owe it to myself to quickly complete the match between Frederica and Sir James after having so long intended it. As you know, flexibility of mind is not an attribute I'm desirous of obtaining."

"But...shouldn't you think more of yourself, your own interests?"

"Excuse me?" When surprised this is a manner of asking, what?

"Why not leave Frederica to the misery of that romantic tender-heartedness which will punish her for the plague she's given you. Secure DeCourcy for yourself—surely it's more in your interest to be well-established yourself than to sacrifice everything for the sake of an ungrateful child. My dear, you are far too concerned for the interests of others—not enough for your own."

Susan considered this carefully.

"There is something in what you say."

"I have another reason to say it: Manwaring's in town."

"Manwaring! How is he, the divine man?"

"Absolutely miserable about you and jealous of DeCourcy—to such a degree I can't answer for his not committing some great imprudence such as following you to Churchill—"

"Heavens!" Lady Susan exclaimed, according to this account.

"I think I dissuaded him from it," Alicia said. "If you do take my advice and marry DeCourcy, it will be indispensable for you to get Manwaring out of the way. Only you have the influence to send him home."

Partial truth is Falsehood's fiercest bodyguard. It might be conceded that portions of the above conversation *could* have occurred as described; as very good friends, Lady Susan and Alicia had a private language and habit of mind that can be described approximately by the term "humourous." They liked to spoof the cant and sentiment of those conforming to Society's insincere verities and the result could be coruscating. But to cite these remarks, out of their context and as if reflecting the true beliefs of two admirable women, is false-witness of the most damnable sort.

★ ★ ★ ★
★ ★ ★

Frederica Vernon had remained at Churchill while her mother was in London. Reginald DeCourcy had stayed also. A strange distance, a barrier, had risen between them, different than the wall of Reginald's indifference before. On Frederica's side a sense of guilt followed her betrayal of her mother and her own solemn promise in appealing to Reginald in the disloyal way she had done. Almost certainly it was this guilt and worry which took her to the Churchill church* that day.

Frederica followed the path through the woods and brambles to get to the church, perhaps unwittingly seeking to punish herself as an occasional thorn pulled at her cloak or scratched her hand. The cloud-covered sky was dark and getting darker, threatening a downpour, with some drops beginning to fall before she reached the shelter of the small church.

The storm had already begun when the young curate, Thomas Edward Braddock,** noticed Frederica sitting silently in the pew just under the stained glass window.

"Miss Vernon? What a pleasure to see you here."

The affable young curate, small of stature but neither imperious nor argumentative, approached her.

"Have you any need of assistance?"

"Yes, thank you... There was a matter regarding which I

---

* The reader might recall that Sir James, on arriving at Churchill, had looked for but not seen the church. He could hardly have been expected to have detected it. Dating from the Seventeenth Century, the Churchill church was more chapel in scale and lay in a dale, separated from the rest of Churchill's park by a high stone wall and a wood, rendering it quite invisible from the road.

** No relation to Gen. Edward Braddock (1695–1755), commander-in-chief of British forces in North America at the start of the French and Indian War, defeated and killed at the Battle of the Monongahela.

wanted to ask: How, in accord with Christian teaching, should the Fourth Commandment be honoured?"

"The Fourth Commandment? Yes—'Remember the Sabbath day, to keep it holy.'"

"No," Frederica said, "I meant the commandment 'Honour thy father and mother...'"

"Oh, the Fifth Commandment! My favourite!" he exclaimed cheerfully. "It's the Church of Rome that has it as the Fourth—yes, the Fifth Commandment: 'Honour thy father and thy mother: that thy days may be long upon the land which the Lord thy God giveth thee.' Beautiful, profound—I believe one should apply this sentiment of Gratitude and Loyalty to every aspect of our lives. We are not born into a savage wilderness but into a beautiful mansion of the Lord that the Lord and those who have gone before us have built. We must avoid neglecting this mansion but rather glorify and preserve it—as we should all of the Lord's Creation. The superb Baumgarten has outlined the aesthetic trinity as 'Truth,' 'Beauty,' and 'Good.' 'Truth' is the perfect perceived by reason; 'Beauty,' by the senses; and the 'Good' by moral will."

Frederica rather lost track of time speaking with the curate, whose erudition and enthusiasm she found comforting. Here was a young man who might have been a truly sympathetic companion over a long life. Could Frederica have imagined becoming Mrs. Thomas Edward Braddock? In fact she did not consider it, or not consider it much; her heart and head were filled with thoughts of another...

★ ★ ★ ★ ★

Emerging from the wooded path on her walk back to Churchill she encountered Reginald. He had a look of surprise, as if he had entirely forgotten her existence, which he nearly had.

"From where do you come?" he asked.

"Church."

"Why were you in church?"

"Well...it is our religion."

Reginald smiled. "Yes, of course, but this time of day—neither morning prayer nor vespers?"

Seeking to avoid a fuller, or truer, explanation Frederica mentioned the usual pretext, that of weather.

"The sky had clouded over," she said. "I was sure there would be a downpour."

"There was," Reginald replied and shook water from his cloak.

Frederica now noticed that he was sopping wet, that he must have been caught in the storm. He dripped water from hat and coat.

"Oh, you are quite drenched: You must put on dry clothes!"

Frederica, approaching as if to protect him from the wet, lightly touched his coat, then jerked her hand back as if it had been burning hot rather than damp.

"Excuse me!" she said, embarrassed and discomposed, immediately starting off to the house ahead of him. Reginald DeCourcy was left to ponder just what had happened before continuing in her wake.

★ ★ ★ ★ ★ ★

References have been made to our Christian faith, a subject many are loath to broach: The faiths of others, in their particulars, are often disconcerting if not dismaying to discover; at other times astoundingly tedious. A great felicity of properly-ordered divine worship is the occasion it provides for a numerous congregation to recite the same prayers, pronounce the same liturgy, sing the same hymns, declare the same credo—to make a beautiful picture of harmony out of the rank odor of their individual beliefs, often heretical or absurd.

The main paths to faith are two,* with the great divide between those whose faith represents a continuum of practice and belief, with no identifiable experience of conversion or spiritual rebirth, and those who have had such an experience. In recent years it has been thought that Science poses a challenge to Christian belief that is unprecedented and, perhaps, unanswerable. In fact, though, laxity and skepticism were far graver threats to the church in the last century, not even considering the outpouring of nauseating Deist mumbo-jumbo in that period. In earlier times Roman and barbarian swords were greater challenges still. Nevertheless, confronted with Science's challenges to our dogma, some Christian thinkers have advanced—mistakenly, I believe—what they consider proofs of the truth of Christian teaching. In this I would say that they are "barking up the wrong tree."** Faith, by its very definition, means going beyond evidence.

---

* Theologians advocating a more particular delineation contend that there are, rather, five.

** The reference is to a dog or dogs barking at the base of a tree, erroneously considering their quarry "tree'd"—i.e., up the tree; here the expression is used as a theological metaphor to create a more vivid image. Another canine metaphor—"This dog won't hunt"—describes a perplexing phenomenon: some dogs will not hunt.

The "Stride of Faith"

For those whose faith is not a continuum from their earliest, pre-rational years it is argued that there must be a "Leap of Faith." This expression, originally the "Leap *to* Faith," now takes the prior form, such deterioration in the precision of our language being now too common to require comment. In either form this image of a "leap" is disturbing. It suggests danger: leaping from one cliff to another, with an abyss below. Searching for and finding faith should not be so compared: One is striding towards a heavenly destination, not diving into or near an abyss. This word itself—"abyss"—is it not weird? Does it not itself suggest evil, by the very sequence of letters? Has a word ever been odder? (Here I refer to words of modest length; among lengthy words certainly strange ones can be found: Mississippi. Or: Antidisunitarianism.)

The great Calvin has taught us* that such dramatic images,

---

* Jean Calvin (born Jehan Cauvin), 1509–1564, French theologian & pastor. His *Institutes of the Christian Religion* (1536) is undoubtedly the greatest work of theological thought, of this millennium, at least.

terrifying "leaps," fraught "rebirths," evidence the vanity of Man rather than the sovereign power of God. We may, we should, we must regenerate; but, of our own volition, we do not "leap" any-where. We should be able to become faithful Christians without any jumping, or terrifying leaps, involved at all. Rather than "Leap of Faith"—with the vanity and self-dramatizing that that suggests—what is needed is a long, hopeful stride, the so-called "Stride of Faith." Certainly a great distance is to be covered, but it should not involve the risk of a terrifying fall into a rocky abyss. With the Stride of Faith our brothers of the "continuum of faith" also stride with us; with the Stride of Faith we seek to regenerate our selves (our souls) while moving forward towards a destiny which only the Almighty will decide. This idea of a Stride of Faith has greatly reassured me and I hope it might do the same for the reader.

A Return to Parklands

Not long after Lady Susan departed Churchill the Vernons also left, journeying with their children and Frederica to visit the elder DeCourcys in Kent. Arriving at Parklands Catherine left the children with their grandfather to find her mother who was just then descending the stairs.

"Oh, Mother!" Catherine embraced her, almost in tears.

"How good to see you—what joy your letter gave us!"

"I wrote too hastily—"

"What?"

"I couldn't imagine that every expectation I had would be so quickly dashed."

"You frighten me!"

"You are right to be frightened. I despair of ever gaining the advantage of that woman—"

"Lady Susan?"

"Her powers are diabolical—"

"Diabolical?!"

"Yes. Just after I wrote I was astonished to see Reginald come from her rooms—the quarrel between them made up! One point only was gained: Sir James Martin's dismissal. Reginald took me aside to give an explanation only Lady Susan could get a man to believe, then Lady Susan did the same. Her assurance, her deceit— my heart sickened. As soon as I returned to the parlour, Sir James' carriage was at the door and he, merry as ever, took his leave. So easily does her Ladyship encourage or dismiss a Lover!"

"But sweet Frederica?" Lady DeCourcy asked. "What of her?"

"Our only consolation! I hope you will love her as much as we do…"

"But when might we know her?"

Catherine turned back to the hall. "Frederica, come—my mother is anxious to meet you."

Frederica, separating herself from her cousins and their grandfather, shortly appeared.

"Mother, I would like to introduce our niece, Frederica. Frederica, let me present my mother, Lady DeCourcy."

"My dear child," the older women said, "I am so pleased to know you. We had such high regard for your late father—and have heard altogether so much in your favour."

"Thank you, Lady DeCourcy—I also have long wanted to meet you and know Parklands about which my cousins often speak."

Their young voices were soon calling Frederica back, joined by Sir Reginald's.

"You may go to them, my dear. We will talk more later; we have a great deal to discuss."

"Thank you, Lady DeCourcy!"

"She is *lovely*," Lady DeCourcy pronounced after Frederica left.

"The poor girl," Catherine said. "Her one chance to break

free... Who knows what punishment her mother will now impose? And the torment Frederica must feel seeing Reginald back under her mother's rule."

"Reginald cannot be blind to such a lovely girl."

"He has been rendered blind: Reginald is more securely Lady Susan's than ever."

"Please don't tell your father," she told Catherine. "I fear for his constitution."

The older man, whose hearing might not have been as bad as everyone assumed, appeared from around the corner.

"Tell me what?"

Oppressive tyrants of the domestic sphere such as the female DeCourcys will always, it seems, portray themselves and their favourites as the "harmed" rather than the "harming." But, we must note, it is not Lady Susan who dedicated herself to maligning others.

Far too many are those who take at face value any slur or accusation, without considering the truth and honesty of the source. In the case of the DeCourcys and their spinster amanuensis, the truthfulness was nil, as the following exercise in character-assassination shows. The malicious authoress presents an absurdity, Lady Susan riding in a carriage (the one my uncle had provided) to Edward Street where she has Alicia Johnson rushing down the front steps to intercept her:

"Susan! Stop!"

"What is it, you funny creature?"

"The worst thing imaginable—Mr. Johnson's been cured!"

"How is that possible?"

"It's this terrible gout of his: No sooner had he heard you were in London than he had a cure. It was the same when I wanted to visit the Hamiltons—then, when I had a fancy for Bath,* nothing could induce him to have a symptom."

"I must intercept Manwaring before he arrives."

"You summoned him here? How very bold, my dear!"

"Could you do me the greatest favour?" Susan asked. "Go to Seymour Street and receive Reginald there. I dare not risk his and Manwaring's meeting; keep him with you all evening if you can. Make up anything; I allow you to flirt with him as much as you like—you'll not find it hard."

"What an intriguing plan—"

"But don't forget my true interest: Convincing Reginald he can't remain in London, for the usual reasons—propriety, his family, and so forth."

★ ★ ★ ★ ★

She next portrays the friends together the day after; the interview between Reginald DeCourcy and Mrs. Johnson has already taken place—the location, the well-appointed parlour of Lady Susan's rooms at Upper Seymour Street.

"At first he was very gloomy," Alicia said. "He couldn't understand why you hadn't come, plying me with questions, some rather awkward. But I spoke ceaselessly of your devotion and admiration—"

"Good."

---

* This alone shows the account's falsity; it suggests that Alicia would have tried to lure Mr. Johnson to Bath when it was well known that it was Tunbridge Wells which he favoured.

"And very quickly he was in good humour. My dear, I see what you mean: How flattery alters a man's spirits. It's delightful. I blush to think of the superlatives I hurled at his head—but which he accepted without demur—"

"When it comes to flattery, don't hold back," Lady Susan commented ("her experience extensive," the spinster wrote). "Men are such gluttons for praise, it's never enough. Much better a Manwaring, sufficiently high in his own regard not to need bolstering from others!"

"How was the charming man?"

Susan smiled.

"I will not deny the real pleasure seeing him afforded me, nor how strongly I felt the contrast between his manners and Reginald's. For an hour or two I was even staggered in my resolution to marry Reginald."

A look of worry passed over Alicia's countenance; Lady Susan explained herself:

"I quite despise that doubting, suspicious cast of mind, where one is always being called on to justify oneself. I immensely prefer the open-hearted, open-handed manner of a Manwaring—even if only his wife's fortune allows it."

"Is Manwaring aware of your intentions?"

"Heavens no! It's essential he not be! I represented Reginald as no more than a trivial flirtation. In fact, we had a good laugh about it. Manwaring was tolerably appeased—oh, to have a few more months with the divine man before submitting to prudence..."

"You worry me, my dear."

"I worry me. Though I detest imprudence, and sincere emotions of all kinds, where Manwaring is concerned..."

I will shortly expose the falsity of this account.

* ★ * ★ * ★ *

Reginald arrived by carriage not long after. Lady Susan accompanied him to the drawing room.

"I am sorry I could not be here to greet you but did I not provide a charming substitute?"

Reginald said nothing, as if in a kind of pout.

"How strange: You remain silent but Mrs. Johnson could not stop singing your praises."

"Excuse me?"

"I fear Alicia has quite fallen in love with you; it's given me quite a scare."

"You're joking."

"But you did like her?"

"Of course—"

"I so admire Alicia: Her husband, Mr. Johnson, is older and disagreeable, but a word of complaint never drops from Alicia's lips. Exemplary. Only by one's friends can one truly be known; that Alicia is mine will, I hope, help you think better of me."

"I already think well of you."

"You were not 'plagued by doubt'?"

"Some things disconcerted me: That you were not here, that—"

"Please, Reginald, don't be severe—I can't support reproaches..."

"But—"

"No, I entreat you, I can't support them. My absence was to arrange a matter so that we might be together. I'm forbidden to say more; please don't reproach me."

"Have you considered what I asked?"

"I have, and since have had time for reflection: I believe

our affairs require a delicacy and caution which, in our candid enthusiasm, we have perhaps insufficiently heeded—"

"What do you mean?"

"I fear our feelings have hurried us to a degree which ill accords with the views of the world. In becoming engaged we were...hasty, unguarded."

"Unguarded?"

"So many friends continue opposed. It's understandable that your family would prefer you marry a woman of fortune: Where possessions are extensive the wish to increase them still further is, if not entirely reasonable, too common to excite surprise. The indelicacy of an early remarriage might also subject me to the censure of those you hold dear."

"I'm sure, in time—"

"Perhaps, but with feelings as poignant as ours..." Lady Susan hesitated.

"You no longer wish to marry?" Reginald reacted as if stung.

"No, no, no. All I'm saying—or hesitantly suggesting—is that we postpone an open understanding until the opinion of the world is in more accord with our own inclinations."

"When might that be?"

Susan considered the question a few moments before replying.

"Let's allow the feelings of our friends to be our guide."

"That could mean never!"

Reginald stood as if about to resume his pacing.

"No. Perhaps...months," Lady Susan replied. "I confess delay is against my every inclination."

"Then let's—"

"No, I can't be responsible for dividing your family."

"I thought we had decided," Reginald said, sitting down again but closer. Reginald might here seem like a weak and pouting fellow but I venture that no man, even Manwaring, would look admirable in such circumstances.

"I know; the prospect of such delay seems insupportable, especially if we were both in London. With separations, only those that are also geographical can be reasonably tolerated."

"What?"

"I'm sorry, Reginald: Staying in London would be the death of our reputations. We must not meet. And not to meet, we must not be near. Cruel as this may appear, the necessity of it will be evident to you."

"Where will you go?"

"It is necessary that I remain in London—there are arrangements that I must make so that we can be together. On the contrary I know your family craves your company—especially that elderly gentleman to whom you owe so much. I would never want to be the cause of an *éloignement** between you and your father, who—forgive me—might not have long left to him."

Reginald seemed surprised: "There is no reason for worry that I know of—Father is rather in his prime."

"Oh, thank Heavens!" Susan said. "So, he's not in decline?"

"He has the usual aches and pains but is overall, I believe, in good health. In any case he would not want any concern on that account—which he would consider so much rubbish."

"Ah, mortality! Our mortality and that of others—but particularly our own—this is the hardest and most implacable hand life deals us. I long to meet the dear gentleman. Of course

---

* *Éloignement,* as has been mentioned, French for estrangement, separation, distancement.

it's natural he would ignore or minimize the cold, sad end that awaits us."

"Not at all. Father's a Christian, for whom the prospect of the end is neither sad nor cold."

"Ah, yes!" Susan agreed. "Thank Heaven for our religion! So important to us in this life, and especially in the next..."

"Must we really wait? I entreat you to reconsider."

At the interview's end Lady Susan asked Reginald to carry, on her behalf, a letter marked "strictly private" to Mrs. Johnson at Edward Street. The task would also give Reginald the opportunity to thank Alicia for her hospitality the prior evening.

The Manwarings of Langford

Lord and Lady Manwaring of Langford, important players in these events, have as yet only been fitfully mentioned. Lucy FitzSmith, an heiress who lost her parents at an early age, had been Mr. Johnson's ward. Though she was not pretty of face, her silhouette was striking and just the sort to provoke the base passions of some men. So it was perhaps not solely her fortune which attracted Lord Manwaring.

Edward Manwaring resembled Lady Susan's late father, the Earl, in habits and manner if not looks. There could be no comparing the shape of their eyes, but they both had the aristocratic knack for losing whatever funds came to hand. Like Mrs. Cross' late husband, Mr. Cross, Lord Manwaring "invested"—but his investments were in horses and cards rather than tottering Scottish banks or plummeting East India Company stock. The end result was the same, but Manwaring's enjoyment was far more: Horses are beautiful, their speed striking, while worthless notes and certificates make poor souvenirs.

Cards and the vagaries of chance have long fascinated the grand and, for us as boys, Lord Manwaring was grandeur defined, grandeur deified, evident in his every look and movement, even the fold of his clothes. As a friend of Uncle James and long resident at Martindale, he was often seen but rarely heard. This silent manner greatly impressed the young: One imagined great thoughts not being expressed; normally one's elders speak too much. My young cousin Frederic Martin hero-worshipped Manwaring and even grew to resemble him physically—admiration and emulation sometimes having that effect.

Whatever qualities Lord Manwaring did have were lost on Mr. Johnson, for whom order, propriety, and respectability were life's objectives and from which he veered only once. Mr. Johnson was expert in detecting the irregularities on a balance-sheet, a circumstance not favourable for Miss FitzSmith's suitor. The cult of "Respectability" now dominant in our land but then still in its infancy, has, in my view, little to do with our Christian faith. Mr. Johnson opposed his ward's engagement from interested motives, matters of income, rent, and debt. Upon her marrying Manwaring he resolved to "throw her off" forever and this estrangement lasted well over two years.

Lord Manwaring had not really minded his wife in the early months of their union; she, in turn, had been careful not to alienate him, even inviting his younger sister, Miss Maria, to stay at Langford. Though Miss Manwaring was not the easiest young lady with whom to get along, Lady Manwaring managed to do so. So perhaps it is true that it was Lady Susan's sojourn at Langford that started the spiral into jealousy and unreason that finally put Lady Manwaring's marriage, and mind, in jeopardy.

The day before Lady Susan met with Reginald, Lady Manwaring had arrived in London with two servants in tow and her mind unhinged. The next afternoon she arrived at the Johnsons' in Edward Street shockingly discomposed.

"I'm in such a state! Excuse me, I don't know what to say..." she said, a sob rising in her throat. "Is Mr. Johnson at home? I must speak with my Guardian!"

"Yes, yes, of course. You poor dear! I'll let him know you're here."

Alicia led her into the salon and opened the door to Mr. Johnson's library.

"Lucy Manwaring is here to see you..."

"Mr. Johnson!" Lady Manwaring howled and lunged past Alicia into the library. "You must help! You must help me! Manwaring's left!"

"Yes, please go in," Alicia said and closed the door, but bent her ear to the conversation within:

"Dear Lucy, please, calm yourself," Mr. Johnson was saying. *"Here, take a seat."*

"He's with her now!"

"Tell me what's happened."

"Manwaring's left! He visits her!"

Alicia was still leaning close to the door when William, the footman, entered.

"Madam, Mr. DeCourcy."

Reginald appeared.

"Oh, good day."

"Mr. DeCourcy!"

Though taken aback by Reginald's inopportune arrival, she moved quickly to intercept him.

"What a surprise to see you!" she said. "So kind of you to call."

"I must thank you for last evening," Reginald said, "for setting matters right. Lady Susan has explained everything. I'm ashamed to have spoken as I did. It was foolish of me—"

"No, no, not at all—most sympathetic," Alicia said, manoeuvring to block his further advance. "But you didn't have to come to thank me; courtesy did not dictate it."

"In fact it's not my sole motive: Lady Susan has entrusted me with a letter for you."

Reginald proffered it with an elegant gesture.

" 'Strictly private,' " Alicia read. "How intriguing."

At this point a scarcely-human, high-pitched plaint pierced the door.

"Has an animal been injured?!" Reginald asked in alarm.

"Private theatricals. *Medea*," Alicia said, citing the Greek play.★ "They perform next week but prefer not to be watched rehearsing," she added while escorting him towards the door, away from the library. "Thank you again for the charming evening."

At precisely this moment Lady Manwaring burst from the library, followed by Mr. Johnson.

"She's with him now!" she wailed. "This can't continue! It mustn't—"

"Lucy, please don't!" Mr. Johnson urged. "Stay here, rest, recover your equanimity—"

"Equanimity!? They're together now!" Lady Manwaring grasped Mr. Johnson's hands. "I implore you—come with me, talk with Manwaring, reason with him. As my Guardian, won't you help?—"

"Even if I found them, what good could be done?"

★ Euripides' *Medea*. A Fifth-Century B.C. play, concerning the barbarian woman who married Jason of the Argonauts, far too gruesome to recount. Remarkable that it should still be performed, but crude melodrama has always had its public.

Alicia stepped in their direction, "Yes, heed Mr. Johnson, his counsel is excellent in such matters—"

"What have you? A letter in her hand?!" Lady Manwaring shrieked and lunged to snatch it from her.

"Return that letter, Madam!" Reginald exclaimed. "It is not for you."

Lady Manwaring was already breaking the letter's seal.

"Lucy, no!" Mr. Johnson called. Both gentlemen still adhered to the code of respecting the confidentiality of correspondence— just before disgracefully abandoning it.

With a quick movement Reginald took the letter from Lady Manwaring.

"Excuse me, Madam, but I believe you were on the verge of making a grave error. You are Lady. Manwaring? Lady Manwaring of Langford? You have undoubtedly recognized your friend Lady Vernon's hand and assumed the letter is for you—"

"My friend? You think that lady is my friend?! She's with my husband now; as we speak, he visits her!"

"That is impossible, Madam. I have just left her; she is entirely alone, even her servant sent off."

"Owen!" Lady Manwaring called.

Another Johnson footman led Lady Manwaring's servant into the drawing room.

"Owen, come here," she said. "Stand here. Tell this gentleman what you saw."

"Your Ladyship..." Owen looked at a loss.

"Repeat to him what you told me."

Obediently Owen turned to address Reginald.

"Well, Sir, Lady Susan sent her servant away, and then you

left. And a few minutes later Lord Manwaring arrived and was received by her Ladyship."

"Alone?" Reginald asked, shaken.

"Yes, Sir, I believe so. No one else came or went."

Lady Manwaring snatched the letter from Reginald and started devouring it like a voracious beast. (Many years later Mrs. Johnson described the scene to me, saying she remembered it as if it were "the day before yesterday." This evocative expression has stayed with me over the years.)

"No—stop, Madam! The letter is for Mrs. Johnson only!"

"Here," Lady Manwaring said, reading: " 'I send Reginald with this letter—keep him there all evening if you can; Manwaring comes this very hour.' "

"That's not possible," Reginald protested.

"I must stop this!" Lady Manwaring turned again to Mr. Johnson: "Please, Sir, come with me."

"What could possibly be gained? It could even be dangerous; this is a matter for your solicitors." Mr. Johnson turned to Alicia: "Mrs. Johnson, this goes beyond what I could imagine: You promised to give up all contact with this woman."

In the heated circumstance it would have been difficult for Alicia to explain the private language of joke and facetiousness the two friends shared. Instead she fell back on what has been termed the "lunacy defense": representing Lady Susan as demented, her letter senseless.

"I have no idea what she writes!" Alicia said. "She's gone mad!"

"I'm sorry to say, my dear," her husband icily replied, "the Atlantic passage is very cold this time of year."

Alicia looked stunned; Lucy Manwaring rescued her from

more searching interrogation by resuming her hysterical crying and fleeing the room.

* * * * *

As soon as she could, Alicia left by carriage for Lady Susan's rooms on Upper Seymour Street. Lady Susan had descended to greet her.

"Agonies, my dear!" Mrs. Johnson exclaimed.

"What's happened?"

"The worst circumstances imaginable. Disaster—"

"'Disaster'?"

"Mr. DeCourcy arrived precisely when he should not have—Lucy Manwaring had just forced herself into Mr. Johnson's study to sob her woes."

"Has she no pride, no self-respect?"

"None. What an impression she makes—bursting from Mr. Johnson's library wailing like a struck child. Seeing the letter in your handwriting, she tore it from Reginald to read aloud—"

"No!"

"Yes. 'Manwaring comes this very hour'!"

Lady Susan turned to lead the way upstairs, but the friends were in such natural sympathy they fell in together and climbed in unison.

"And Reginald heard that?"

"He read it himself."

Lady Susan looked amazed.

"How ungentlemanly! Shocking! I can't believe it."

"Yes," Alicia agreed. "Very shocking."

"A gentleman, entrusted with correspondence marked 'private,' reads it regardless—and then, because of some confidential remarks, the obloquy is mine! But who has acted badly in this affair? Only you and I stand innocent of reading other people's correspondence!"

"Unluckily Lady Manwaring also wormed out of her servant that Manwaring visited you in private."

"Oh." Lady Susan was briefly silenced. "Facts are horrid things!"

They continued up the stairs and, within several steps, Lady Susan had recovered her equanimity. "Don't worry. I'll make my story good with Reginald. He'll be a little enraged at first but I vow that, by dinner tomorrow, all will be well."

Alicia looked more doubtful.

"I'm not sure...He was with Mr. Johnson when I left. Forgive me for saying it but...I dread to imagine what's being said in your disfavour..."

At this point, rather than worry for herself, Lady Susan was characteristically concerned for her friend:

"What a mistake you made marrying Mr. Johnson, my dear: too old to be governable, too young to die!"

* * * * * *

There is an idiomatic expression which dates not from that era, but from our own, predicated on knowledge of man's bipedism: "Then the other shoe dropped." As regards Reginald "the other shoe" dropped the next day when he came to pay his final call upon Lady Susan. She was writing at her *escritoire* when her maid showed Reginald into the drawing room. He announced himself icily: "Good evening, Madam."

"Finally you come."

"Only to bid you farewell."

Lady Susan received this with a smile: "What do you mean?"

"I think you must know."

"No," she said.

"The spell is broken. All is revealed. I now see you as you are."

"Charming, but I'm starting to find this manner of yours irritating."

"Since I left yesterday I've received such a mortifying account of the true facts of your history as to make clear the absolute necessity of an immediate and eternal separation between us."

"You make me laugh." But she did not, in fact, laugh.

"You can't doubt to what I allude."

"I do doubt. Have I ever concealed anything from you? I'm utterly bewildered."

"Langford," Reginald said, almost in a groan. "Langford... Langford. The word alone should be sufficient."

"No, it is not... The word 'Langford' is not of such potent intelligence for me."

Reginald remained silent and pacing.

"You agitate me beyond expression! Such moodiness and suspicion are not, I think, worthy of a young man of your distinction."

"It is from Lady Manwaring herself that I've learned the truth."

"'The truth'? What possible connection can there be between Lady Manwaring and 'truth'? She's entirely deranged. You must have seen that."

"Her servant witnessed Manwaring's visits here."

"That servant, Owen, is notoriously defective in understanding. Did Owen explain what prompted Manwaring's visits? Their entirely innocent and blameless nature?"

"If you recall the regard I had for you, you must realize the agony I felt reading your words."

"Then I would advise you to stop reading other people's correspondence! Alicia has a droll humour. Everything we write is inverted and in-joke; she delights in curious phrasing only we can decipher. Of course it would seem outlandish or shocking to others—we don't expect others to read our correspondence and don't put things for their benefit."

This exactly matches what I understood and have explained regarding the conversations and correspondence between Alicia and Lady Susan. So much for those who doubted my account!

Lady Susan continued: "Manwaring only visited me as his wife's friend—"

"'Friend'?" Reginald rudely replied. "She herself denies that."

"Of course—I was her friend when she was sane, her great enemy since. Manwaring only left Langford to escape her deranged suspicions. In granting him an interview my sole motive was to persuade him to return to her, to see what might be done to ease the poor woman's mind—"

"But why 'alone'? Why did you arrange to see him alone?"

"What do you mean?"

"You sent away your servant."

"You can't divine my motive there?" Lady Susan looked quickly to see if the door were closed before continuing. "Servants have ears, with the unfortunate tendency to repeat whatever they imagine they hear. I dreaded injuring the poor lady's reputation still further."

Maud, the young woman Lady Susan had engaged as parlour maid during her London stay, just then did have her ear to the door but, hearing Lady Susan's words, prudently withdrew; she later confessed this to my uncle's valet. Meanwhile the truth of Lady Susan's observation cannot be overstated: Great care should be taken as to what is said before servants, even when they are apparently distant. This remains true to our day.

"You imagine I could accept such an explanation?" Reginald asked, as disbelieving now as he was credulous before.

"I can only tell you what I know to be true."

"Did you succeed?"

"What?"

"Did you convince Manwaring to return to his wife?"

"Yes, I did. But it seems her judgement is too deteriorated to allow it. Her suspicious and jealous state is not of a nature to accept reassurance."

"You forget, I saw the letter with my own eyes—"

"No, I don't forget. I greatly resent it—a fault you compounded by misinterpreting what you should never have seen. Do you think I would confide a letter to a third party if I thought its contents in any way dangerous? Haven't I already explained everything which the ill-nature of the world might interpret in my disfavour? What could so stagger your esteem for me now? After all we've discussed and meant to one another, that you would again doubt my intentions, my actions, my word..."

To this Reginald remained silent.

"I'm sorry, Reginald. I've reflected deeply upon this: I cannot marry a man of an untrusting disposition. I cannot have it."

"What?"

"We cannot marry. Whatever commitment there was between us is severed; any connection impossible."

"What are you saying?" Reginald asked, stunned by her changed tone, a slight tremulousness in his voice.

"Mistrust does not bode well for any union. I have a great regard for you—yes, a passionate one. But that I must master. It's not tolerable to be constantly made to defend oneself."

Reginald stood still for a time, then, eyes watering, bowed and left.

★ ★ ★ ★ ★
★ ★

Parklands was located in the west of Kent, reached by carriage without difficulty, so the extreme fatigue and low spirits Reginald DeCourcy exhibited upon his return might be ascribed to factors other than a tiring journey. His arrival was a *soulagement*★ for his mother, though; she hurried to find Catherine to impart the news.

"Catherine! Catherine!" Lady DeCourcy called, approaching the stairway as Catherine descended it. "Reginald's returned!"

"He's here?"

"Yes, he's just gone to find your father."

"It's not—"

"No, the most happy news—our fears were in vain."

"What?"

"The engagement's off!"

"How?"

"Lady Susan broke it off herself."

"She did?" Catherine looked apprehensive.

"Reginald is most cast down. But I trust he will recover before too long and—dare we say—cast his look elsewhere?"

Rather than sympathy for her brother, or pleasure at her own apparent "victory," Catherine chose instead to pursue her strange *vendetta*.★★

"That woman's a fiend!"

★ *Soulagement* (French), relief, respite, solace, consolation.
★★ *Vendetta*, a term for revenge-seeking from a blood feud, said to have originated in my father's native Corsica but in fact imported from Italy. From the Latin *vindicta*, as in *vindictive*.

"What do you mean?"

"Lady Susan. She has an uncanny understanding of men's natures. By forcing the rupture herself she has engaged Reginald's pride."

A look of confusion crossed Lady DeCourcy's face.

"Uncanny? I don't understand..."

"Reginald will start to doubt everything he has heard to her detriment; a guilty regret will overwhelm him. Slowly, surely, he will convince himself he has wronged her."

"You frighten me!"

"You are right to be frightened: If Frederic Vernon, renowned for good sense, let Lady Susan ruin him—what chance has Reginald?"

"You speak as if your brother were not wise; I am sure he is. Everyone comments on his lively intelligence."

"You are the best of mothers, but Reginald has just the sort of sincere nature most vulnerable to a woman of her genius—"

"You think she's a genius?"

"Diabolically so, like the serpent* in Eden's Garden."

"Does this woman always get her way?"

"From what I understand only clever tradesmen are astute enough to see through her stratagems; several banded together to send their agents to intercept her on Seymour Street, obliging her to pawn the last of her jewels."

Shortly Reginald and his father joined them, Reginald most cast down while the old man's spirits were correspondingly high.

---

* A Biblical character, cited in Genesis 3, actually Satan in disguise. The Biblical commentator Matthew Henry states: "He [Satan] is the great promoter of falsehood of every kind. He is a liar, all his temptations are carried on by his calling evil good, and good evil, and promising freedom in sin."

"Slay the fatted calf, my dear—the prodigal's returned!" He looked to Reginald. "What's wrong, my boy? The joy of seeing your aged parents eludes you?"

Perhaps made uncomfortable by the menace of confrontation, the threat of sharp words between father and son, Lady DeCourcy had left the room—though, as it turned out, that was not the circumstance.

"Don't tease him, Father," Catherine said.

"Teasing our children is a father's right!"

"But you will have him fleeing back to London."

"No risk of that, I assure you," Reginald said, finally breaking his silence. "London holds no charm for me."

"Oh, you've realized that," his father said. "Good. Never appealed to me at all. Dirty, noisy—noxious gases, soot...I don't see the point of towns. Far better to live on one's own land. Everyone should."

"I'm afraid this relates to my sister-in-law," Catherine said.

"Yes, sister—congratulations on your entire vindication."*

"On the contrary, I don't see you out of danger at all."

"'Danger'? I assuredly am."

"What's all this about?" Sir Reginald asked. "What's happened? I don't understand."

At this moment Lady DeCourcy re-entered with a sheaf of music and a blushing Frederica.

"Reginald dear," his mother said. "Frederica's prepared a charming piece—help me persuade her to sing it for us."

"Oh, no!" Frederica said. "You're too kind, Lady DeCourcy. I'm not ready—"

"Excuse me, Miss Vernon, Mother," Reginald said. "As

---

* From the Latin *vindicatio*.

much as I'd like to hear it, I am afraid I am too tired to be a suitable audience. So, if you'll excuse me—"

"No, you must stay!" Sir Reginald exclaimed. "Frederica's a songbird—never heard anything like it…Don't deny us this pleasure, my dear. Reginald, we need you to insist."

"Well, as I said, I—"

"No, I'm sorry," Frederica said, embarrassed. "Excuse me."

"You must let us hear you, my dear," Lady DeCourcy insisted. "Please—"

"The 'Kentish Nightingale,' I call her," Sir Reginald added. "Voice's remarkable, even to my hearing."

"She must have that from her mother's side," Reginald reflected with a slight, lovelorn tremolo. "Lady Susan's voice is a clear, natural soprano. Lovely, beautiful…"

"Oh, it is, is it?" his father responded.

Hearing voices from the front of the house, Catherine asked, "Did you expect visitors, Mother?"

"No…Who would visit us?"

Footsteps could now be heard in the hall, followed by Charles Vernon's arrival, a cordial smile on his cheerful face.

"Look who's come from London," he said, extending his arm in a welcoming gesture. "What an agreeable surprise!"

A beautiful woman in traveling clothes appeared and stood still for a moment at the edge of the grand room; the DeCourcys, who had all turned towards her, stood as if frozen in place.

"What a delightful family pose!" Lady Susan happily exclaimed.

"Yes, it is the season for families to unite, so it is especially welcome to have you here."

"Thank you, Charles!" Susan said, and then turning to Sir

Reginald and Lady DeCourcy continued: "I do hope that, recognizing a mother's anxiety to see her child, you might excuse the abruptness of my arrival."

"Nothing to excuse," Charles insisted. "Sir Reginald, Lady DeCourcy—might I introduce my sister-in-law, Lady Susan Vernon..."

"*Enchantée,*" Lady Susan said. "Please forgive this intrusion, but now that I am fixed in town I cannot rest with Frederica away."

"Isn't such anxiety new?" Catherine asked.

Susan, ever cheerful, replied: "Yes, it is—I entirely agree, dear sister. But now I am in London where the instruction Frederica needs can so readily be found. Her voice has some promise—"

"Some?" Sir Reginald said. "She is a veritable songbird. The 'Kentish Nightingale,' I call her."

"Do you? Is this really Kent?" Susan glanced quickly towards the window. "Delightful," she pronounced. Then, speaking slowly and raising her voice to accommodate the old man's hearing, she continued: "You are right, Sir—Frederica has the native talent a bird might... But those few notes can get repetitive."

"But, Mother," Frederica asked, "couldn't I stay?"

Lady Susan smiled. "'But, Mother, couldn't I stay?' Charming." Then, turning to Catherine, she added: "I thank you, dear sister, for making Frederica feel so at home and welcome..."—with a nod to the DeCourcys—"...wherever she goes."

To Frederica she added: "I've secured you a lesson with Signore Veltroni. Where the 'Grand Affair of Education' is concerned, there's no excuse for half-measures!"

Speaking loudly again to Sir Reginald, she asked: "Isn't it key, Sir, to cultivate her voice? A 'nightingale,' didn't you say?"

Sir Reginald, a little befuddled and intimidated by this apparition, conceded: "Yes, that's right. The 'Kentish Nightingale,' I call her."

"A delightful appellation, Sir," Susan agreed. "And perhaps, with a teacher such as Signore Veltroni, it could even become true... Frederica, have you your things?"

"Leave for London now?" Lady DeCourcy protested. "We had so looked forward to having Frederica with us."

"How remarkable," Lady Susan observed. "Only a few weeks ago it was hard to find anywhere for Frederica, and now the World fights for her company! Astonishing."

"Astonishing that she was neglected then, or is fought over now?" Catherine asked.

"An excellent observation, dear sister—but I will stop now, because I know my daughter hates to be praised." She then politely greeted Reginald: "How are you, Sir? I hope well." Then, turning to Frederica, added: "We should go, my dear."

"Excuse me, Mother, I must collect my things."

"Yes, you must! We can't buy a new wardrobe for each displacement..." Susan left with Frederica to help pack her things. The others, stunned, watched them go.

"The poor girl," Lady DeCourcy said. "Did you see her face?"

Catherine said: "I must talk to her and remind her that she will always have a home with us."

"Or with us," her mother said, looking to Sir Reginald.

"If you are referring to the past," Charles said, "I doubt her mother will again risk misinterpretation. Henceforth we can rest assured that Lady Susan will make clear to Frederica the consideration and affection which guide her actions."

* * *
* * *

Returned to London, Lady Susan immediately visited Alicia. The friends' only concession to Mr. Johnson's prohibition was to avoid the house itself and instead stroll the sculpted paths of the Johnsons' garden where their conversation might also be far from servant ears.

"Miss Maria Manwaring is just come to town to be with her aunt, armed with a new wardrobe," Alicia warned, "vowing she will have Sir James before she leaves London again."

"We shall see! I have not been idle, my dear—nor gone to the trouble of retrieving Frederica from Parklands to again be thwarted. Let Miss Maria Manwaring tremble for the consequences! She may sob, Frederica whimper, and the Vernons storm—but Sir James will be Frederica's husband before the winter's out!"

"You brilliant creature!"

"Thank you, my dear. I am done submitting my will to the caprices of others; resigning my own judgement in deference to those to whom I owe no duty and feel little respect. Too easily have I let my resolve weaken: Frederica shall now know the difference!"

"You're too indulgent with the girl—why let Frederica have him, when you could grab him yourself?"

"Sir James?"

"Yes. I know your unselfish nature—but can you afford to bestow Sir James on Frederica while having no Sir James of your own?"

An initial look of surprise crossed Lady Susan's face, then a dark look.

"Are you insulting me?"

"Just the opposite, my dear: I don't doubt your ability to get DeCourcy whenever you want him, but is he really worth having? Isn't his father just the sort of enraging old buzzard who will live forever? How would you live? On the allowance that Frederica, as 'Lady Martin,' might grant you? As a guest at Churchill? I would rather be married to my own husband than dependent on the hospitality of others."

For a long spell they walked in silence. Susan once started to speak, then stopped. Alicia looked to her.

"You make a point," Susan finally conceded.

In my view, this entire episode is ludicrously implausible. My aunt, as I knew her, was wholly free of material concerns.

As the reader has perhaps noticed, great care has been taken with the punctuation used in this account. For me, as regards literature, punctuation is what separates true greatness from the merely good—and certainly from the false. I would commend the reader to glance (no more) at the spinster's mendacious account included as an appendix to this volume; even a cursory look will show the gross carelessness of her attention to punctuation. Can someone so careless of the rules of punctuation—known to everyone and most apparent in the breach—be counted upon to strictly adhere to truth in the absence of such direct surveillance? I think not.

Generally speaking, the more punctuation, correctly used, the better and more precisely truthful is the literary production, in my opinion. A sentence without a mark of punctuation every ten to twelve words, or so, even if just a comma, should be considered suspect, or highly dubious; most important, though, is the correct use of the semi-colon.

When I was at Westminster School, where I had followed in
my uncle's footsteps (though Sir James was rusticated from Westminster in his fifth-form year, the only student to be "sent up"
rather than "sent down" from the school, he bore it no grudge,
which was characteristic of his sanguine and forgiving temperament), a favourite master, Mr. Grove, liked to say that if we
learned to master the semi-colon we could expect to be success-
ful in whatever path we chose in life. One might easily accept
this as true as to the Church or the Law, where language and
correct punctuation are crucial, but Mr. Grove argued with considerable vehemence that proper use of the semi-colon would
lead to great success in any endeavour, including business. We
were surprised by his insistence and, when not in his presence,
mocked him for it.

Yet over the intervening years I have learned that what we
are taught by our elders, no matter how seemingly improbable
or ridiculous, is nearly always true. From the very start of our
firm we found that well-punctuated business letters, including
semi-colons properly used, inspired confidence in both custom-
ers and creditors; it would be hard to imagine the Barings bank
confiding us with such large loans had it been otherwise. As Mr.
Grove had predicted, success came quickly. Our company,
Martin-Colonna & Smith, soon achieved and for a considerable
time maintained a leading position in the rare and precious
woods trade prior to the sudden and unexpected collapse of the
mahogany market, which no one could have foreseen.

I should also touch on the very interesting (to me at least)
subject of articles of speech. As Mrs. Johnson, a sparkling con-
versationalist despite her American origins, once asked me,
"Mr. Martin-Colonna, which article of speech would you say
you prefer?" I had no hesitation in answering her: "Without a

doubt, the definite one." I value precision and clarity, in articles of speech as well as in punctuation; the definite article ensures both. With our Empire's vast expansion across the globe as well as our involvement in world trade, we now must communicate with many peoples less fluent in our language, sometimes not fluent at all. The indefinite article risks misinterpretation. Whether we are trading in Burma, Jamaica, India, Trinidad, or America, the definite article is clearer and apt to be better understood. Relying on indefinite articles when speaking with the natives of foreign and exotic lands can be dangerous, leading to misinterpretations of authority and command. "The" is rarely misunderstood.

This concern with precision has often led me to pronounce punctuation in speech to achieve the greatest possible clarity. I strive to mention the form of a pause, or stop, or appositive clause, whichever is desired. Enunciating punctuation involves quite a lot more effort, but whatever helps comprehension will, I believe, ultimately be rewarded. I approve the pains Sir Reginald took in pronouncing the punctuation when he read Catherine's letter to Lady DeCourcy, though her failure to appreciate it was typical of that family.

However, I fear this effort to be precise through spoken punctuation greatly hurt my case at the trial. I had thought that achieving full clarity would have been appreciated and valued by the court and judicial authorities. Not at all. I was gravely mistaken.

"Now, now—that's enough of that!" Judge Wilkinson exclaimed in the midst of my testimony, cutting me off with shocking rudeness. I found this comment so outlandish, coming from the bewigged, black-robed jurist, I could not at first comprehend his words.

"Excuse me, your honour, what is 'enough of' what?" The testimony was transcribed by a court reporter and I now have it before me: "Now, now—that's enough of that!" Not an elegant or learned formulation, nor the proper way to address a gentleman in court, as if he were a governess addressing a dim or unruly child.

I cannot regret my attempt to achieve clarity, even if unorthodox, though I am afraid that my honest attempt to improve court practice was held against me at the time of sentencing, which Mr. Knox, the barrister, considered especially harsh. I asked if he thought my attempt at precision, specifying the punctuation in my testimony, was unwise, but he was reluctant to reply. When I pressed him he finally said, "Perhaps unwise—though admirable, brave, astute—but we seem to have run up against a clear prejudice: that punctuation should be seen but not heard. You are an idealist, Sir!"

I was gratified that Mr. Knox, for whom I have considerable respect, appreciated my intention even if it did not meet with success and has made my stay in this sinister place longer than it might have been otherwise.

Parklands to London

Weeks later, at Parklands, Catherine Vernon put aside a letter she had been studying.

"I despair at learning anything from these letters," she told her mother. "They look to have been written under maternal supervision."

"Poor Frederica. Poor, dear Frederica!"

"We must get her back to Churchill."

"Or Parklands—your father adores his 'Kentish Nightingale.'"

"To think that, at any moment, she might be brow-beaten into marrying that Martin! We must protect her: not just for her own sake but for her dear, late father's."

"But what can we do?"

"We must find the argument that will persuade her mother that it is in her own interest, which is of course her only guide. That will mean going to London; fortunately Charles must have some business or other there to justify such a trip."

"What a marvellous husband you have, my dear; Charles seems to live to oblige."

"It is true, I have been lucky—Charles always seems to have some pretext or other for doing just what's wanted."

Charles Vernon could then be heard approaching from the hallway. Reaching the DeCourcy mother and daughter, he stopped, his smile tinged with a slight look of apprehension.

"Dearest," Catherine began, "I believe you have pressing business in London."

"Oh, yes," Charles said with a smile, and it was true that he usually had business there of some kind or other.

★ ★ ★ ★ ★ ★ ★

At Upper Seymour Street Lady Susan received the Vernons warmly, herself leading them up the stairs towards the drawing room.

"You're so kind to visit!" she said. "Frederica will be delighted. How are the children—especially my dear Frederic?"

"Very well, thank you," Catherine said.

Susan called up the stairs, "Frederica, come see who's here!" To the Vernons, she continued: "I cannot express my gratitude for the hospitality you've extended us."

"Not at all," Charles replied. "Our great pleasure."

"Frederica?"

Frederica appeared at the top of the stairs and slowly descended, seeming to have reverted to her former timid state.

"Hello, Frederica," Catherine greeted her with a warm smile.

"Good afternoon, my dear," Charles said. "I hope you are well."

Frederica curtsied and seemed to blossom, as a flower might, though more daisy than rose.

"Thank you—it's so good to see you!"

"Frederica," her mother said, "why don't you go and get your music? Select something charming to show your aunt and uncle what you've studied."

"With pleasure," Frederica replied with a bow and left.

"Mind your head," Lady Susan warned Charles, who was exceptionally tall, as they entered the drawing room; he, fortunately, took the precaution, ducking in time. Concern for the welfare of others was habitual with Lady Susan and, perhaps for that reason, insufficiently appreciated, which I have sought to correct here.

"You will see the strides she's making," Lady Susan said. "Frederica plays all the new music: Haydn, Hummel, Bernardini*...Cherubini**...Please, do sit down."

The Vernons made themselves comfortable on the large sofa of neo-classical design.

"So, you are happy with her progress?" Charles asked.

Lady Susan considered the question. "Yes," she said finally. "Only in a city such as London, I believe, could she have had such instruction."

This intelligence depressed the Vernons' hopes; Charles turned to Catherine.

"If Frederica is making such good progress in London— well, that complicates matters..."

"What complication would that be?" Susan asked.

"We had hoped Frederica might return to Churchill," Charles said.

---

* Marcello Bernardini (c. 1740–c. 1799), Italian composer.
** Luigi Cherubini (1760–1842), pronounced "Carubini," Paris-based Italian composer known for his choleric disposition. "Some maintain that his temper was 'very even' because he was always angry." —Adolphe Adam

"She's greatly missed," Catherine added. "By the little ones especially—"

"What a moving sentiment of cousinly regard! My concern, my obligation, is to see the defects in Frederica's education repaired."

"Could we invite one of her teachers to Churchill to continue her lessons there?" Charles asked.

"What a kind thought," Susan said. "These, however, are not teachers but rather London's most sought-after masters; no invitation to a country retreat, even such a delightful one as Churchill, is likely to be in their power to accept."

"Perhaps a private tutor then—"

"I must confess something," Lady Susan said. "Frederica and I have become such great friends I would find it hard to part with her. You might have noticed that, for a time, there was a strange tension between us. That has now happily disappeared. You can imagine how pleased I am—"

Catherine seemed to slump in her seat.

"Excuse me, are you well?"

"I'm sorry—we had so set our hearts on Frederica's return."

"I understand completely. She's turned into an agreeable companion—even her tendency towards extreme quiet I have grown to find soothing." Glancing first towards the door, Lady Susan added: "One factor does concern me: Do you think she looks quite well?"

"Oh, yes," Charles replied too quickly, his habitual agreeableness closing off a possible line of argument for Frederica's return to Churchill.

"That was your impression?" Susan asked. "London's vaporous air is not, I worry, quite healthy for her. Doesn't she seem pale?"

"She does," Catherine said. "The London air, these smoky gases, cannot be salutary for a girl her age. Fresh, country air is what the young require."

"Yes...How curious they are."

"Let her come visit then—"

"I'm not able to express my sense of such kindness—yet, for a variety of reasons, I'm reluctant to part with her."

For a moment an awkward silence descended, broken by Charles.

"But," he said, "does not the town's dank air favour the spread of influenza?"

"The influenza? In London?" Lady Susan asked, alarmed.

"Several cases have been reported—it is, after all, the season for it."

"Of all the disorders in the world the risk of an influenza contagion is what I most dread for Frederica's constitution," Lady Susan confessed.

"Shouldn't we consider then removing her from that danger?" Catherine asked.

"What you say gives me pause...But it would be such a hardship to lose my daughter's companionship just as I've come to rely on it—and of course her studies..."

★ ★ ★ ★ ★

Among the carriages kept by the Johnsons was a charming two-horse landau which Alicia preferred for travel within London. This now pulled up before Lady Susan's door on Upper Seymour Street with Susan shortly leaving the house to join her friend. As Susan took her seat opposite Alicia, the coachman gave the order for the horses to start and, with a jolt, the carriage pulled away.

"Congratulate me, my dear! Frederica's aunt and uncle have taken her back to Churchill."

"But I thought you had grown to enjoy Frederica's company so."

"Comparatively. A bit. But I am not so self-indulgent as to want to wallow in the companionship of a child."

"Alas," Alicia said. "I fear this is our last meeting—at least while Mr. Johnson is in life. His business at Hartford has become extensive. If I continue to see you he vows to settle in Connecticut forever."

"You could be scalped!!" Susan exclaimed. "I had a fear that the great word 'Respectable' would one day divide us. Your husband I abhor, but we must yield to necessity. Our affection cannot be impaired by it and, in happier times, when your situation is as independent as mine, we will unite again— for this I shall impatiently wait."

"I also."

Susan took Alicia's hands in hers.

"May Mr. Johnson's next gouty attack end more favourably!"

The carriage pulled to a stop near the palatial archway leading to the Hampshire gardens. A tall, handsome man stood in its shadow waiting for them—he now approached them: It was Lord Manwaring.

"Adieu, my friend," Lady Susan said as she stepped from the coach.

The months passed, the weather warmed, the rains paused. Amidst Churchill's shrubbery and blooming flowers Reginald now walked with a lovely and radiant Frederica rather than with her far more beautiful mother. They spoke of Cowper,

Thompson, Addison, and Steele. For both of them the great Pope was a particular favourite.

In the main hall Charles Vernon asked Catherine if she knew where Frederica might be. "Lady Susan has written her."

Taking the letter, Catherine went to look for Frederica and, not finding her, called her name.

"Coming!" Frederica replied as she and Reginald were just then returning from the garden.

"A letter has come from your mother."

"Thank you, Aunt Catherine. What does she write?"

"She has written to you herself."

Frederica took the letter and sat to cautiously break its seal. What was the intelligence that she feared to learn? Frederica read silently for a few moments until a look of surprise altered her countenance.

"My mother and Sir James Martin have wed!"

"What?!" Reginald exclaimed. "How could that happen? How could they possibly marry?"

"To what do you refer?" Charles Vernon asked. "Both were free to do so: he a bachelor, Susan a widow."

"Sir James Martin is a fool!" Reginald said.

"Well, a bit of a 'rattle,' perhaps," Catherine conceded.

"A bit of a 'rattle'? He's a complete blockhead."

"There are three possible explanations as I see it," Charles said. "First, perhaps Sir James has more merit than we have allowed—"

"No," Reginald replied.

"Second, perhaps, in order to secure your future, Frederica, your mother thought it necessary to make a prudent match herself." Charles looked to Frederica for agreement— which she provided.

"That could be the case," she said, thoughtfully. "Mother has always been concerned for my future."

"And the third possible explanation?" Reginald asked.

"That she...came to love him," Charles said. "There is a saying—'the heart has its strangeness,' or words to that effect. The heart is an instrument we possess but do not truly know. Human love partakes of the divine, or at least has in my case."

Charles looked to Catherine, who responded with a sweet, though deceptive, smile. Turning to Reginald he continued: "You will find it in writings of Rousseau—*Julie, or the New Heloise,* I think. I will confirm the citation if you're interested."

"I just find it incomprehensible that so brilliant a woman could marry such a pea brain...or *peas* brain."

"It happens all the time," Charles replied; Catherine smiled.

"It strains credulity," Reginald persisted.

"Certainly—as has been said—Sir James is no Solomon, but if he can give Lady Susan the happiness and security of which the sad events of recent years have deprived her, then he is someone that I and all of us should value."

"I very much agree, Uncle," Frederica added. "We all should—I wish them every happiness in their life together!"

★ ★ ★ ★ ★

In London, at Edward Street, Alicia Johnson faced the daily struggle of contending with her older and difficult husband. He delighted in threats to return her to her native Hartford in the valley of the Connecticut River,★ the upper reaches of which

---

★ As I write I see on my wall a painting of Indian braves paddling a canoe on the upper reaches of that waterway, the only painting the bailiffs left to me. As I understand it, the braves portrayed belonged to the same New England tribe as those who had scalped a cousin of Alicia's at Hadley, Massachusetts, some

were a wilderness area where Indian attacks had been frequent. It is widely known, I believe, that many of our countrymen have a taste for cruelty. Rather than shame, some even boast of this proclivity. Causing pain, humiliating others, making them squirm is keenly enjoyed. In Spain this passion of our compatriots for pain-causing even has a name, "El Vicio Ingles"—the "English Vice," they call it. A posture of superiority or dominance is sought; citizens from other lands, or even our own colonies, are deprecated (which to me, it seems, is somewhat similar to those parents who delight in maligning their own children). For Mrs. Johnson the oppressiveness of her domestic situation was severe; it was marvellous that she was able to maintain her cheerful, humourous manner in the face of it but, then, she was Lady Susan's friend and both women had the genius to remain charming in the least charming circumstances.

When my uncle, recently married, paid her a call that spring, one would have thought her without a worry of any kind. Sir James was in exceptionally good humour as he joined her in her drawing room, decorated in the exquisite style which Robert Adam made famous.*

"Congratulations, Sir, on a match I long favoured," Alicia said amiably. "There's a rightness to your being together—not that any man could really deserve Lady Susan."

"I agree most heartily...And I've the pleasure of adding that double congratulations are in order."

"What?"

---

decades earlier. (Her cousin survived but was compelled to wear an unsightly stocking-cap for the rest of his days.) Such things did happen in that wild land.
* I had the opportunity to know this room myself, having had tea with Mrs. Johnson there in the last year of her life. There is something poignant in becoming acquainted with such a personage shortly before she departed this life.

"The most beautiful woman in England—present company excepted—will soon be the most beautiful mother. Yes, I am to be a father."

"Marvellous! You certainly don't delay matters...Congratulations, Sir!"

A footman brought in the elaborate tea service while Alicia herself took charge of mixing the tea leaves in their canister.

"Yes," Sir James said. "The very morning after the wedding Lady Susan hinted at the happy news—which was shortly confirmed."

"How truly marvellous!"

My uncle's high spirits and good humour were rather infectious.

"I am as proud as you can imagine." The sound of a wheezing sob from another part of the house attracted his attention: "What's that?"

"Such a burden," Alicia whispered. Sir James leaned forward to catch her words. "When Lord and Lady Manwaring separated, Mr. Johnson—who was Lucy Manwaring's guardian—invited her to live with us."

"Really?" Sir James asked. "What upsets her?"

"The separation still. She goes on about it."

"What?"

"All this carrying on about a marriage that ended weeks ago. If a woman fails to please her husband—why go on about it, advertising one's failure? Why announce to the world that the man who knows you best would rather be with someone else?"

"It seems," Sir James observed, "as if Lady Manwaring has failed to consider the difference between the sexes. For a husband to wander is not the same as vice versa. If a husband strays, he is merely responding to his biology—that is how men are made. But…"—the idea made Sir James smile—"…for a woman to act in a similar way is ridiculous, unimaginable. Just the idea is funny: hew, hew, hew…hew, hew."

"I couldn't agree more, quite funny…"

They both sat.

"I rather blame Lady Manwaring's scene-making for driving her husband away," Sir James said. "But her loss has been our gain. As a result of all the trouble her solicitors caused, we have had Manwaring with us these past weeks."

"That's not inconvenient?"

"Not at all! Capital fellow. Couldn't get on better—loves to hunt, small and large game. Excellent to have a guest and the talk which comes with it. Of course Lady Susan's sharp, but it's easier to talk with a fellow, particularly one who shares one's interests…Before long we'll have another guest."

"Frederica?"

Sir James laughed. "No! Of course, the baby."

At precisely this moment the door burst open; Lady Manwaring, distraught and disheveled, entered.

"Manwaring? Manwaring? Have you seen my husband?" Lady Manwaring asked in a tone of feverish passion, her voice breaking. "What have you been saying, Sir?! Tell me. How… is he?"

"Well, Madam, very well, I believe. Couldn't be better."

Unable to bear this happy report, Lady Manwaring sobbed and left the room. While Sir James and Mrs. Johnson certainly had sympathy for her distress they were too polite to show it.

"Tea?" Alicia asked.

"Quite," Sir James replied, resuming his seat.

A Wedding

My own first visit to Churchill was to play a highly visible role in Frederica and Reginald DeCourcy's wedding. After her engagement, when Frederica came to Martindale to visit her mother (Reginald thought it best to absent himself from this trip), she asked whether my brother and I might be part of the wedding party as flower boys or, rather, train-holders, or some such. It seems to me that the young children included in a wedding party are there in an essentially decorative mode; the actual work is not hard.

The Churchill church was, as has been mentioned, more chapel- than church-like; it was not far from the Churchill house but obscured from the road leading to it by a wood, a high stone wall, and a discrepancy in the terrain's elevation. The wedding was small and the first guests already arriving when Sir James' carriage pulled up, then rolled back, almost knocking down an elderly couple passing behind it. "Careful!" the man called angrily to the driver; it is true that such sudden movements can lead to dismemberment or death.

My uncle stepped down from the carriage, followed by Lady Susan, large with child at this time, as well as Lord Manwaring.

Sir James was delighted to finally see the Churchill church—missing which had so disoriented his first visit, leading to the eternal, cruel mocking of the DeCourcys. "So—here's the Church!" he said with his characteristic ebullience. "But, where's the hill? Don't see it." He looked around, squinted and looked further. "There doesn't seem to be one—strange. Odd."

The young curate of the Churchill church conducted the wedding with distinction. Frederica Vernon and Reginald DeCourcy were wed and nearly everyone appeared pleased, though it was certainly Reginald who had the better half of the bargain. Afterwards, as the wedding party passed under the garland arch, little Charlotte Vernon called out, "God bless you all!" Her cordial spirit suggested she was her father's rather than her mother's child. I was jealous that I had not thought to call out something similarly striking; in any case she came to a bad end.

The wedding was followed by a delicious wedding breakfast at Churchill's main hall. While the other children ran about inanely outside I remained within, closely observing what went on, as well as sampling the dishes. I as yet had no idea that I would one day write this book, so I cannot claim to have specifically overheard these conversations; but I do have Frederica's wedding memory book to draw from as well as my own extraordinary (as Mrs. Johnson called it) ability to imagine just how everything was, even in those circumstances when I could not have been present (though in this case I was).

First, Charles Vernon suggested to Frederica that Lady Susan "must be very proud" of her.

"I am enormously grateful to her also," Frederica replied. "Without my mother's efforts I would not have found such happiness." She glanced to where her mother, splendid with child, stood speaking with Sir James and Lord Manwaring; the conversation in that group was reciprocal.

"You must be most proud of Frederica," Sir James offered.

"I would not say 'proud,'" Lady Susan specified. "That is not a word I favour. I will say that I am glad that I was able to attend to Frederica's education. My daughter has shown herself to be cunning and artful—I could not be more pleased: A Vernon shall never go hungry."

Elsewhere Catherine Vernon spoke with the young curate of the Churchill church. "And bearing false-witness?"

Could it be that a consciousness of guilt and pang of regret stirred in a DeCourcy breast? "That would be the Ninth," the young curate replied.

So, it turns out that those who so mocked my uncle for misconstruing the commandments did not know them well either. *"And why beholdest thou the mote that is in thy brother's eye but considerest not the beam that is in thine own eye?" (Matthew 7:3–5).* To my knowledge no DeCourcy has ever answered that question.

Meanwhile Lady DeCourcy urged Charles and Sir Reginald to help her convince Frederica to sing. "That would be delightful," Charles said. "The 'Surrey Songbird,' we call her."

"What? No!" Sir Reginald exclaimed. "She's the 'Kentish Nightingale'—always call her that. 'Surrey Songbird'—nonsense, rubbish...ridiculous!"

As Wilson, the butler, announced the wedding couple, the guests turned to where Reginald and Frederica stood on the set of steps leading to Churchill's "new" wing, built two centuries before.

"Over the past months," Reginald said, "I have continued to be startled by Frederica's loveliness and good heart. I had wanted to write some verses as a memorial to these discoveries, but they are now so extensive they would form a volume, so I will read just these few lines." Reginald started reading from a loose paper.

> *Blest tho' she is with ev'ry human grace,*
> *The mien engaging, and bewitching face;*

"Mien engaging?" Sir Reginald asked Charles sotto voce.

"Yes," Charles replied. "'Mien'—appearance or countenance—from the French 'mine,' I believe. I could find you the citation."

After a look of admiration, or great regard, towards Frederica, Reginald continued:

> *Yet still an higher beauty is her care,*
> ***Virtue,*** *the charm that most adorns the fair;*
> *Long may they those exalted pleasures prove*
> *That spring from worth, constancy and love.*

Re-reading these verses now, decades later, I am struck by their quality. The question arises, were they Reginald DeCourcy's own, or might he have found "inspiration" from other sources? In any case, when he concluded, those present applauded his (or someone's) beautiful composition.

"As you may already know," Frederica said, "I take Lady DeCourcy's requests as commands...Therefore, I will sing this piece."

Frederica paused, searching for the right tone, then began her song, first hesitantly then in beautiful voice, far preferable

in my opinion to the over-praised, irritating cheep-cheep of
the nightingale:

> *Over the mountains*
> *And over the waves,*
> *Under the fountains*
> *And under the graves,*
> *Under floods that are deepest,*
> *Which Neptune obey*
> *Over rocks that are the steepest,*
> *Love will find out the way.*

If the allusions and images ("Neptune") in the opening
stanza of this ancient, traditional air now sound rather fanciful
to our ears, the next stanza was perhaps more pertinent.

> *You may esteem him*
> *A child for his might,*
> *Or you may deem him*
> *A coward from his flight.*
> *But if she, whom Love doth honour,*
> *Be concealed from the day*
> *Set a thousand guards upon her,*
> *Love will find out the way.*

With Frederica and Reginald's marriage, and the immi-
nent birth of my cousin Edward Martin, this history has largely
concluded. The reader will perhaps appreciate the restraint I
have exercised in removing myself from the narrative. Many,
though, have urged me to recount my own part of this story,
that I relate something of my connection to it and my own

history from which I have hitherto refrained, with a few punctual exceptions.

The vindication of my aunt, Lady Susan Grey Vernon Martin, has, I believe, been entirely accomplished. But other important propositions remain to be addressed.

Perhaps the first should be self-evident and is so except in the minds of the bigoted: *Merely to be in prison does not make one a criminal.* Incarceration is not some certain, invariable, tell-tale sign of evil-doing, or anything of the kind. Certainly the ignoble abode from which I now write is not where I intended to reside at this stage of my life. Yet, while humiliating, the series of events—or, occasionally, lack of event—which led to my arrival here does not paint the dire picture that the small-minded—or nasty-minded, such as the DeCourcys—might describe.

In fact the entire controversy regarding my financial and legal difficulties involved at most three matters. The first and perhaps the easiest to explain was that which related to the Barings bank loan. Martin-Colonna & Smith, the joint stock company which Smith* and I had begun for the importation of rare and precious woods, prospered almost immediately. Year after year sales mounted, with shipments of rare woods that were ever more abundant and precious. After the disappointment of my law career I was pleased to discover that I had a certain "genius for business." Scarcity and demand indicated the trajectory of the precious woods trade could only continue upward, so we envisioned expansion. The respected and highly reliable Barings Brothers endorsed our plans, partners Thomas Baring and Russell Sturgis

---

* Mr. Thomas Smith, my late partner, no connection with Mr. Charles Smith, the slanderer and gossip-monger.

taking a particular interest, which was highly gratifying to us. Barings approved a substantial loan to enable the firm to purchase woods on a far larger scale. The first setback was the discovery of insects of a boring kind in a shipment of teak from Rangoon (detritivores, especially dangerous for rare woods). What dramatically undercut our expansion plans—which were reasonable, precise, and well-laid and of which I remain immensely proud— was the unforeseen collapse of the mahogany market, which no one anticipated or could have done. The laws of scarcity and demand dictated that the direction of prices for this remarkably valuable and handsome wood—properly cut, treated, and polished, it is strikingly beautiful, with dark, ingrained patterns fascinating to contemplate—could only increase. To have thought otherwise would have shown a complete disregard for what the great Adam Smith★ has described as the law of the market.

The change in attitude of our bankers at Barings, who had seemed such good fellows and whom we had considered friends, was striking and rather chilling. I will accept that perhaps I did not have sufficient assets to sign a personal note guaranteeing repayment of the loan in the event of default—but who could have anticipated such an eventuality? I do not believe anyone could have though the bank documents seemed to have made detailed provision for such an eventuality, which, I must say, I now greatly resent.

Second, at the law chambers with which I maintained a connection—perhaps against my better judgement but not

---

★ Adam Smith (1723–1790), philosopher of political œconomy. As the reader is probably aware, Smith (no relation to Thomas or Charles) was a member of Dr. Johnson's Literary Club which included among its members Dr. Charles Burney, father of Fanny Burney, later Madame D'Arblay, whose epistolary novels the spinster authoress sought to ape.

wanting to leave our clients without reliable advice—there were some simple and easily resolvable problems regarding the escrow and trustee accounts. I have never bragged or boasted of expertise in the clerical or bookkeeping area, and if Messrs. Sampson, Thales, and West had shown more patience, I am convinced everything could have been resolved without recourse to drastic and insulting procedures.

These matters will be sorted out one day, but my friendship and respect they have lost forever.

Finally, I have to stand corrected as to the meaning of the term "co-mingling" which I understood as referring to something quite different. I had every intention of restoring the funds as soon as the price of mahogany again turned upwards, which I had reason to believe it soon would.

Suffice it to say that all those who were supposedly "injured" by my alleged actions or inactions are going about their lives essentially as before, while I am punished and humiliated. That my vindication will ultimately come and be complete I am certain. At that point, if still alive, I will take a glass of port wine and think pleasant thoughts, taking pride in never having myself been vindictive or a tattletale.

Like my uncle I prefer to see life's goblet not as half-empty but as adequately-filled, adapted well for portability or, perhaps, for raising in an enthusiastic toast, without the spills and mess and ruined clothes an entirely-full goblet would almost certainly occasion.

As I see it, while the door to triumph in the rare woods trade has closed, the door to literature has opened.

The True Account of Lady Susan Vernon, Her Life & Loves

By a Lady

A Note on the Title: Four fair copies of this account were circulated in manuscript among the DeCourcys' intimates, then among their acquaintances, and so on, until an extensive readership had been reached. The objective: to damage as far as possible an admirable Lady's reputation. The addition of the phrase "Her Life & Loves" is to suggest scandal where there was none, or comparatively little.

Calling this farrago of misrepresentation a "True Account" is the boldest of libels. The author meanwhile hides her identity under the mask of anonymity, a privilege not afforded her victim, whose actual name is announced in the very title.

A "Table of Contents" listing forty-one letters was added to give the work an air of veracity. Most of these letters, in fact, never existed. The version which the printer, Mr. John Murray, has chosen to include is the last she prepared, in which she turned her account of this history (already decidedly false) into the "epistolary" form then fashionable, despite (or perhaps attracted by) the additional level of falsity added: the contortions and anachronistic affectation required to transform conversations and scenes of life into an "exchange of letters."

Not long after this work acquired its initial notoriety, the great Sir Walter Scott published his epic *Marmion,* with the memorable lines below appearing to reflect directly upon it:

Marmion, Canto VI. Stanza 17:

Yet Clare's sharp questions must I shun
Must separate Constance from the nun
Oh! what a tangled web we weave
When first we practise to deceive!

The anonymous Lady's false "account" is published here the same way a physician might seek to heal a wound by expelling its pus.

Table of Contents

★ In my opinion this Table of Contents is not especially useful and, in fact, quite tedious. However, the "Genealogical Table," which bears some interest, has been corrected and placed at the head of this volume [see page xi].

Letter 1

Lady Susan Vernon to Mr. Vernon.
Langford, December.

My dear Brother

I can no longer refuse myself the pleasure of profiting by your kind invitation, when we last parted, of spending some weeks with you at Churchill, & therefore, if quite convenient to you & Mrs. Vernon to receive me at present, I shall hope within a few days to be introduced to a Sister whom I have so long desired to be acquainted with. My kind friends here are most affectionately urgent with me to prolong my stay, but their hospitable & chearful dispositions lead them too much into society for my present situation & state of mind; & I impatiently look forward to the hour when I shall be admitted into your delightful retirement. I long to be made known to your dear little children, in whose hearts I shall be very eager to secure an interest. I shall soon have need for all my fortitude, as I am on the point of separation from my own daughter. The long illness of her dear Father prevented my paying her that attention which Duty & affection equally dictated, & I have too much reason to fear that the Governess to whose care I consigned her was unequal to the charge. I have therefore resolved on placing her at one of the best Private Schools in Town, where I shall have an opportunity of leaving her myself, in my way to you. **I am determined, you see, not to be denied admittance at Churchill. It would indeed give me most painful sensations to know that it were not in your power to receive me.**

Yr. most obliged & affec: Sister
S. VERNON.

Note on Letter the First: *The Anonymous Lady's account has been "salted" with a few actual letters in the same way that those touting the sale of shares in fraudulent mines "salt" them with quantities of valuable ore. Yet, like the counterfeiter who cannot stop, she adds two menacing lines at the letter's end that Lady Susan never would nor could have written.*

I bestowed a little notice, in order to detach him from Miss Manwaring; but if the World could know my motive _there_, they would honour me. I have been called an unkind Mother, but it was the sacred impulse of maternal affection, it was the advantage of my Daughter that led me on; & if that Daughter were not the greatest simpleton on Earth, I might have been rewarded for my Exertions as I ought.

Sir James did make proposals to me for Frederica; but Frederica, who was born to be the torment of my life, chose to set herself so violently against the match that I thought it better to lay aside the scheme for the present. I have more than once repented that I did not marry him myself; & were he but one degree less contemptibly weak, I certainly should, but I must own myself rather romantic in that respect, & that Riches only will not satisfy me. The event of all this is very provoking: Sir James is gone, Maria highly incensed, & Mrs. Manwaring insupportably jealous; so jealous, in short, & so enraged against me, that, in the fury of her temper, I should not be surprised at her appealing to her Guardian, if she had the liberty of addressing him—but there your Husband stands my friend; & the kindest, most amiable action of his Life was his throwing her off forever on her Marriage. Keep up his resentment, therefore, I charge you. We are now in a sad state; no house was ever more altered: the whole family are at war, & Manwaring scarcely dares speak to me. It is time for me to be gone; I have therefore determined on leaving them, & shall spend, I hope, a comfortable day with you in Town within this week. If I am as little in favour with Mr. Johnson as ever, you must come to me at No. 10 Wigmore Street; but I hope this may not be the case, for as Mr. Johnson, with all his faults, is a Man to whom that great word "Respectable" is always given, & I am known to be so intimate with his wife, his slighting me has an awkward Look.

I take Town in my way to that insupportable spot, a Country Village; for I am really going to **Churchill.** Forgive me, my dear friend, it is my last resource. Were there another place in England open to me, I would prefer it. Charles Vernon is my aversion, & I am afraid of his wife. At Churchill, however, I must remain till I have something better in view. **My young Lady accompanies me to Town, where I shall deposit her under the care of Miss Summers, in Wigmore Street,** till she becomes a little more reasonable. **She will make good connections there, as the Girls are all of the best Families.** The price is immense, & much beyond what I can ever attempt to pay.

Adieu, I will send you a line as soon as I arrive in Town. —

Yours Ever,
S. VERNON.

Note on Letter the Second: *As can be seen, the many interpolations greatly alter the letter's tone and meaning. Here, in contrast with the prior letter, it is the actual words which are marked in bold.*

Letter 3

Mrs. Vernon to Lady De Courcy.
Churchill.

My dear Mother

I am very sorry to tell you that it will not be in our power to keep our promise of spending our Christmas with you; & we are prevented that happiness by a circumstance which is not likely to make us any amends. Lady Susan, in a letter to her Brother, has declared her intention of visiting us almost immediately — & as such a visit is in all probability merely an affair of convenience, it is impossible to conjecture its length. I was by no means prepared for such an event, nor can I now account for her Ladyship's conduct; Langford appeared so exactly the place for her in every respect, as well from the elegant & expensive stile of living there, as from her particular attachment to Mrs. Manwaring, that I was very far from expecting so speedy a distinction, tho' I always imagined from her increasing friendship for us since her Husband's death, that we should at some future period be obliged to receive her. Mr. Vernon, I think, was a great deal too kind to her when he was in Staffordshire; her behaviour to him, independent of her general Character, has been so inexcusably artful and ungenerous since our Marriage was first in agitation that no one less amiable & mild than himself could have overlooked it all; & tho', as his Brother's widow, & in narrow circumstances, it was proper to render her pecuniary assistance, I cannot help thinking his pressing invitation to her to visit us at Churchill perfectly unnecessary. Disposed, however, as he always is to think the best of every one, her display of Greif, & professions of regret, & general resolutions of prudence were sufficient to soften his heart, & make him really confide in her sincerity. But as for myself, I am still unconvinced; & plausibly as her Ladyship has now written, I cannot make up my mind till I better understand her real meaning in coming to us. You may guess, therefore, my dear Madam, with what feelings I look forward to her arrival. She will have occasion for all those attractive Powers for which she is celebrated, to gain any share of my regard; & I shall certainly endeavour to guard myself against their influence, if not accompanied by something more substantial. She expresses a most eager desire of being acquainted with me, & makes very gracious mention of my children, but I am not quite weak enough to suppose a woman who has behaved with inattention if not unkindness to her own child, should be attached to any of mine. Miss Vernon is to be placed at a school in Town before her Mother comes to us, which I am glad of, for her sake &

Letter 4

Mr. De Courcy to Mrs. Vernon.
Parklands.

My dear Sister

I congratulate you & Mr. Vernon on being about to receive into your family the most accomplished Coquette in England. As a very distinguished Flirt, I have always been taught to consider her; but it has lately fallen in my way to hear some particulars of her conduct at Langford, which proves that she does not confine herself to that sort of honest flirtation which satisfies most people, but aspires to the more delicious gratification of making a whole family miserable. By her behaviour to Mr. Manwaring she gave jealousy & wretchedness to his wife, & by her attentions to a young man previously attached to Mr. Manwaring's sister deprived an amiable girl of her Lover. I learnt all this from a Mr. Smith, now in this neighbourhood (I have dined with him, at Hurst & Wilford), who is just come from Langford, where he was a fortnight in the house with her

Ladyship, & who is therefore well qualified to make the communication.

What a Woman she must be! I long to see her, & shall certainly accept your kind invitation, that I may form some idea of those bewitching powers which can do so much—engaging at the same time, & in the same house, the affections of two Men, who were neither of them at liberty to bestow them—and all this without the charm of Youth! I am glad to find Miss Vernon does not accompany her Mother to Churchill, as she has not even Manners to recommend her, & according to Mr. Smith's account, is equally dull & proud. Where Pride & Stupidity unite there can be no dissimulation worthy notice, & Miss Vernon shall be consigned to unrelenting contempt; but by all that I can gather, Lady Susan possesses a degree of captivating Deceit which it must be pleasing to witness & detect. I shall be with you very soon, & am

> your affec. Brother
> R. DE COURCY

Note on Letter the Fourth: *The above letter is an entire fabrication. Mr. Reginald DeCourcy was then on an extended sojourn at Churchill, absent for only a day, and therefore would not have written his sister such a letter, nor with such language—which clearly betrays a female hand. Some of the false accusations here were introduced elsewhere. The spinster authoress, wedded (though otherwise a spinster) to the idea of gaining literary prestige for herself by recasting her account into the then prestigious "epistolary" form used by the great Richardson and Madame D'Arblay, falsified her narrative still further as she turned her* *account of the events into this increasingly awkward and implausible "exchange of letters." For my account (the preceding volume) I have referred to her earlier versions which described the events and conversations directly, though of course laced with her habitual slanders and falsehoods which I have largely, I believe, identified and cauterised.*

Letter 5

Lady Susan Vernon to Mrs. Johnson.
Churchill.

I received your note, my dear Alicia, just before I left Town, & rejoice to be assured that Mr. Johnson suspected nothing of your engagement the evening before. It is undoubtedly better to deceive him entirely; since he will be stubborn, he must be tricked. I arrived here in safety, & have no reason to complain of my reception from Mr. Vernon; but I confess myself not equally satisfied with the behaviour of his Lady. She is perfectly well-bred, indeed, & has the air of a woman of fashion, but her Manners are not such as can persuade me of her being prepossessed in my favour. I wanted her to be delighted at seeing me—I was as amiable as possible on the occasion—but all in vain. She does not like me. To be sure, when we consider that I _did_ take some pains to prevent my Brother-in-law's marrying her, this want of cordiality is not very surprising; & yet it shews an illiberal & vindictive spirit to resent a project which influenced me six years ago, & which never succeeded at last.

I am sometimes half disposed to repent that I did not let Charles buy Vernon Castle, when we were obliged to sell it; but it was a trying circumstance, especially as the sale took place exactly at the time of his marriage; & everybody ought to respect the delicacy of those feelings which could not endure that my Husband's Dignity should be lessened by his younger brother's having possession of the Family Estate. Could Matters have been so arranged as to prevent the necessity of our leaving the Castle, could we have lived with Charles & kept him single, I should have been very far from persuading my husband to dispose of it elsewhere; but Charles was then on the point of marrying Miss De Courcy, & the event has justified me. Here are Children in abundance, & what benefit could have accrued to me from his purchasing Vernon? My having prevented it may perhaps have given his wife an unfavourable impression—but where there is a disposition to dislike, a motive will never be wanting; & as to money-matters it has not withheld him from being very useful to me. I really have a regard for him, he is so easily imposed on! The house is a good one, the Furniture fashionable, & everything announces plenty & elegance. Charles is very rich, I am sure; when a Man has once got his name in a Banking House, he rolls in money. But they do not know what to do with it, keep very little company, & never go to Town but on business. We shall be as stupid as possible. I mean to win my Sister-in-law's heart through the children; I know all their names already, & am going to attach myself with the greatest sensibility to one in particular,

Letter 6

Mrs. Vernon to Mr. De Courcy.
Churchill

Well, my dear Reginald, I have seen this dangerous creature, & must give you some description of her, tho' I hope you will soon be able to form your own judgement. She is really excessively pretty. However you may choose to question the allurements of a Lady no longer young, I must, for my own part, declare that I have seldom seen so lovely a Woman as Lady Susan. She is delicately fair, with fine grey eyes & dark eyelashes; & from her appearance one would not suppose her more than five & twenty, tho' she must in fact be ten years older. I was certainly not disposed to admire her, tho' always hearing she was beautiful; but I cannot help feeling that she possesses an uncommon union of Symmetry, Brilliancy, & Grace. Her address to me was so gentle, frank, & even affectionate, that, if I had not known how much she has always disliked me for marrying Mr. Vernon, & that we had never met before, I should have imagined her an attached friend. One is apt, I believe, to connect assurance of manner with coquetry, & to expect that an impudent address will naturally attend an impudent mind; at least I was myself prepared for an improper degree of confidence in Lady Susan; but her Countenance is absolutely sweet, & her voice & manner winningly mild. I am sorry it is so, for what is this but Deceit? Unfortunately, one knows her too well. She is clever & agreable, has all that knowledge of the world which makes conversation easy, & talks very well with a happy command of Language, which is too often used, I believe, to make Black appear White. She has already almost persuaded me of her being warmly attached to her daughter, tho' I have been so long convinced to the contrary. She speaks of her with so much tenderness & anxiety, lamenting so bitterly the neglect of her education, which she represents however as wholly unavoidable, that I am forced to recollect how many successive Springs her Ladyship spent in Town, while her Daughter was left in Staffordshire to the care of servants, or a Governess very little better, to prevent my believing what she says.

If her manners have so great an influence on my resentful heart, you may judge how much more strongly they operate on Mr. Vernon's generous temper. I wish I could be as well satisfied as he is, that it was really her choice to leave Langford for Churchill; & if she had not stayed three months there before she discovered that her friends' manner of Living did not suit her situation or feelings, I might have believed that concern for the loss of such a Husband as Mr. Vernon, to whom her own behaviour was far from unexceptionable, might for a time make her wish for retirement.

But I cannot forget the length of her visit to the Manwarings; & when I reflect on the different mode of Life which she led with them, from that to which she must now submit, I can only suppose that the wish of establishing her reputation by following, tho' late, the path of propriety, occasioned her removal from a family where she must in reality have been particularly happy. Your friend Mr. Smith's story, however, cannot be quite correct, as she corresponds regularly with Mrs. Manwaring. At any rate it must be exaggerated; it is scarcely possible that two men should be so grossly deceived by her at once.

Yrs. &c. CATH. VERNON.

Note on Letter the Sixth: *As mentioned, Reginald DeCourcy was only away hunting with the Lymans in Sussex for a day. He and his sister would not be exchanging such letters as they were both at Churchill.*

Letter 7

Lady Susan Vernon to Mrs. Johnson.
Churchill.

My dear Alicia

You are very good in taking notice of Frederica, & I am grateful for it as a mark of your friendship; but as I cannot have any doubt of the warmth of that friendship, I am far from exacting so heavy a sacrifice. She is a stupid girl, & has nothing to recommend her. I would not, therefore, on any account have you encumber one moment of your precious time by sending for her to Edward Street, especially as every visit is so many hours deducted from the grand affair of Education, which I really wish to be attended to while she remains with Miss Summers. I want her to play & sing with some portion of Taste & a good deal of assurance, as she has _my_ hand & arm, & a tolerable voice. _I_ was so much indulged in my infant years that I was never obliged to attend to anything, & consequently am without the accomplishments which are now necessary to finish a pretty Woman. Not that I am an advocate for the prevailing fashion of acquiring a perfect knowledge of all Languages, Arts, & Sciences. It is throwing time away; to be Mistress of French, Italian, & German, Music, Singing, Drawing, &c. will gain a Woman some applause, but will not add one Lover to her list. Grace & Manner, after all, are of the greatest importance. I do not mean, therefore, that Frederica's acquirements should be more than superficial, & I flatter myself that she will not remain long enough at School to understand anything thoroughly. I hope to see her the wife of Sir James within a twelvemonth. You know on what I ground my hope, & it is certainly a good foundation, for school must be very humiliating to a girl of Frederica's age. And by the by, you had better not invite her any more on that account, as I wish her to find her situation as unpleasant as possible. I am sure of Sir James at any time, & could make him renew his application by a Line. I shall trouble you meanwhile to prevent his forming any other attachment when he comes to Town. Ask him to your house occasionally, & talk to him of Frederica, that he may not forget her.

Upon the whole, I commend my own conduct in this affair extremely, & regard it as a very happy instance of circumspection & tenderness. Some Mothers would have insisted on their daughter's accepting so good an offer on the first overture, but I could not answer it to myself to force Frederica into a marriage from which her heart revolted; & instead of adopting so harsh a measure, merely propose to make it her own choice, by rendering her thoroughly uncomfortable till she does accept him.—But enough of this tiresome girl.

You may well wonder how I contrive to pass my time here, & for the first week it was most insufferably dull. Now, however, we begin to mend; our party is enlarged by Mrs. Vernon's Brother, a handsome young Man, who promises me some amusement. There is something about him which rather interests me, a sort of sauciness & familiarity which I shall teach him to correct. He is lively & seems clever;, & when I have inspired him with greater respect for me than his sister's kind offices have implanted, he may be an agreable Flirt. There is exquisite pleasure in subduing an insolent spirit, in making a person predetermined to dislike, acknowledge one's superiority. I have disconcerted him already by my calm reserve, & it shall be my endeavour to humble the pride of these self-important De Courcys still lower, to convince Mrs. Vernon that her sisterly cautions have been bestowed in vain, & to persuade Reginald that she has scandalously belied me. This project will serve at least to amuse me, & prevent my feeling so acutely this dreadful separation from You & all whom I love.

Adieu.
Yours Ever
S. VERNON.

Note on Letter the Seventh: *Especially damning, it seems to me, is that nowhere in these letters is there any mention of Lady Susan's friend and companion, Mrs. Cross, who had accompanied her to Churchill and with whom she shared many confidences.*

Letter 8

Mrs. Vernon to Lady De Courcy.
Churchill.

My dear Mother

You must not expect Reginald back again for some time.
He desires me to tell you that the present open weather
induced him to accept Mr. Vernon's invitation to prolong his stay in Sussex, that they may have some hunting
together. He means to send for his Horses immediately,
& it is impossible to say when you may see him in Kent. I
will not disguise my sentiments on this change from you,
my dear Madam, tho' I think you had better not communicate them to my father, whose excessive anxiety
about Reginald would subject him to an alarm which
might seriously affect his health & spirits. Lady Susan has
certainly contrived, in the space of a fortnight, to make
my Brother like her. In short, I am persuaded that his
continuing here beyond the time originally fixed for his
return is occasioned as much by a degree of fascination
towards her, as by the wish of hunting with Mr. Vernon,

& of course I cannot receive that pleasure from the length
of his visit which my Brother's company would otherwise give me. I am, indeed, provoked at the artifice of
this unprincipled Woman. What stronger proof of her
dangerous abilities can be given than this perversion of
Reginald's judgement, which when he entered the house
was so decidedly against her? In his last letter he actually
gave me some particulars of her behaviour at Langford,
such as he received from a Gentleman who knew her
perfectly well, which, if true, must raise abhorrence
against her, & which Reginald himself was entirely disposed to credit. His opinion of her, I am sure, was as low
as of any Woman in England; & when he first came it
was evident that he considered her as one entitled neither
to Delicacy nor respect, & that he felt she would be
delighted with the attentions of any Man inclined to flirt
with her.

Her behaviour, I confess, has been calculated to do
away with such an idea; I have not detected the smallest impropriety in it—nothing of vanity, of pretension,
of Levity; & she is altogether so attractive that I should
not wonder at his being delighted with her, had he
known nothing of her previous to this personal
acquaintance; but against reason, against conviction, to
be so well pleased with her, as I am sure he is, does
really astonish me. His admiration was at first very
strong, but no more than was natural, & I did not wonder at his being much struck by the gentleness & delicacy of her Manners; but when he has mentioned her
of late it has been in terms of more extraordinary
praise; & yesterday he actually said that he could not be

surprised at any effect produced on the heart of Man by such Loveliness & such Abilities; & when I lamented, in reply, the badness of her disposition, he observed that whatever might have been her errors, they were to be imputed to her neglected Education & early Marriage, & that she was altogether a wonderful Woman. This tendency to excuse her conduct, or to forget it in the warmth of admiration, vexes me; & if I did not know that Reginald is too much at home at Churchill to need an invitation for lengthening his visit, I should regret Mr. Vernon's giving him any. Lady Susan's intentions are of course those of absolute coquetry, or a desire of universal admiration. I cannot for a moment imagine that she has anything more serious in view; but it mortifies me to see a young Man of Reginald's sense duped by her at all. I am, &c.

CATH. VERNON.

Note on Letter the Eighth: *The reader might have noted that in her account the authoress flattered her DeCourcy patrons by styling their surname in the aristocratic French manner with the* particule* *"de" separated from the rest of the name. The true origin of the name however was not French but the Irish "Decoursey."*

---

* French term for the use of *de* (French for "from") before a surname, often indicating a pretension to nobility.

Letter 9

Mrs. Johnson to Lady Susan.
Edward St.

My dearest Friend

I congratulate you on Mr. De Courcy's arrival, & I
advise you by all means to marry him; his Father's
Estate is, we know, considerable, & I believe certainly
entailed. Sir Reginald is very infirm, & not likely to
stand in your way long. I hear the young Man well
spoken of; & tho' no one can really deserve you, my
dearest Susan, Mr. De Courcy may be worth having.
Manwaring will storm of course, but you may easily
pacify him; besides, the most scrupulous point of honour could not require you to wait for _his_ emancipa-
tion. I have seen Sir James; he came to Town for a few
days last week, & called several times in Edward Street.
I talked to him about you & your Daughter, & he is so
far from having forgotten you, that I am sure he would
marry either of you with pleasure. I gave him hopes of
Frederica's relenting, & told him a great deal of her

improvements. I scolded him for making Love to Maria Manwaring; he protested that he had been only in joke, & we both laughed heartily at her disappointment; and, in short, were very agreable. He is as silly as ever.—Yours faithfully

ALICIA.

Note on Letter the Ninth: *As I believe has been established, Mrs. Johnson's regard for my Uncle was respectful and affectionate; calling him "as silly as ever" is an obvious, malicious interpolation.*

Letter 10

Lady Susan Vernon to Mrs. Johnson.
Churchill.

I am obliged to you, my dear friend, for your advice respecting Mr. De Courcy, which I know was given with the full conviction of its expediency, tho' I am not quite determined on following it. I cannot easily resolve on anything so serious as Marriage; especially as I am not at present in want of money, & might perhaps, till the old Gentleman's death, be very little benefited by the match. It is true that I am vain enough to believe it within my reach. I have made him sensible of my power, & can now enjoy the pleasure of triumphing over a Mind prepared to dislike me, & prejudiced against all my past actions. His sister, too, is, I hope, convinced how little the ungenerous representations of any one to the disadvantage of another will avail when opposed to the immediate influence of Intellect & Manner. I see plainly that she is uneasy at my progress in the good opinion of her Brother, & conclude that nothing will be wanting on her part to counteract me;

but having once made him doubt the justice of her opinion of me, I think I may defy her. It has been delightful to me to watch his advances towards intimacy, especially to observe his altered manner in consequence of my repressing by the calm dignity of my deportment his insolent approach to direct familiarity. My conduct has been equally guarded from the first, & I never behaved less like a Coquette in the whole course of my Life, tho' perhaps my desire of dominion was never more decided. I have subdued him entirely by sentiment & serious conversation, & made him, I may venture to say, at least _half_ in Love with me, without the semblance of the most commonplace flirtation. Mrs. Vernon's consciousness of deserving every sort of revenge that it can be in my power to inflict for her ill-offices could alone enable her to perceive that I am actuated by any design in behaviour so gentle & unpretending. Let her think & act as she chuses, however. I have never yet found that the advice of a Sister could prevent a young Man's being in love if he chose it. We are advancing now towards some kind of confidence, & in short are likely to be engaged in a sort of platonic friendship. On _my_ side you may be sure of its never being more, for if I were not already as much attached to another person as I can be to any one, I should make a point of not bestowing my affection on a Man who had dared to think so meanly of me.

Reginald has a good figure, & is not unworthy the praise you have heard given him, but is still greatly inferior to our friend at Langford. He is less polished, less insinuating than Manwaring, & is comparatively

Letter 11

Mrs. Vernon to Lady De Courcy.
Churchill.

I really grow quite uneasy, my dearest Mother, about Reginald, from witnessing the very rapid increase of Lady Susan's influence. They are now on terms of the most particular friendship, frequently engaged in long conversations together; & she has contrived by the most artful coquetry to subdue his Judgement to her own purposes. It is impossible to see the intimacy between them so very soon established without some alarm, tho' I can hardly suppose that Lady Susan's views extend to marriage. I wish you could get Reginald home again under any plausible pretence; he is not at all disposed to leave us, & I have given him as many hints of my Father's precarious state of health as common decency will allow me to do in my own house. Her power over him must now be boundless, as she has entirely effaced all his former ill-opinion, & persuaded him not merely to forget but to justify her conduct. Mr. Smith's account of her proceedings at Langford, where he accused her of having made Mr. Manwaring & a young Man engaged to Miss Manwaring distractedly in love with her, which Reginald firmly believed when he came to Churchill, is now, he is persuaded, only a scandalous invention. He has told me so in a warmth of manner which spoke his regret at having ever believed the contrary himself.

How sincerely do I grieve that she ever entered this house! I always looked forward to her coming with uneasiness; but very far was it from originating in anxiety for Reginald. I expected a most disagreable companion for myself, but could not imagine that my Brother would be in the smallest danger of being captivated by a Woman with whose principles he was so well acquainted, & whose character he so heartily despised. If you can get him away, it will be a good thing.

Yrs. affec:ly,
CATH. VERNON.

Note on Letter the Eleventh: *Reference was earlier made to Lady Susan's own account of these events, written in the loose pages of her journal and entirely refuting the authoress' malicious inventions portraying Lady Susan's motives as interested, her character devious.*

I am sorry that I am not now in a position to quote from these pages directly. When the bailiffs came to my rooms before dawn the day after the court decision, pounding on the door so violently I thought it might break, they removed a valuable mahogany chest, finely crafted with small drawers and a secret compartment lined with green felt—precisely where I left the pages of Lady Susan's journal for safe-keeping. I was so groggy,

the chaos so great, the time so short, with many other possessions and personal effects at risk, it was not until the next week
that I realized her journal had been removed with that chest.
By the time I reached the bailiffs' rooms the pages were gone.
Though my memory is considered excellent it is not of the
Daguerreotypic sort, capable of reproducing an exact image
(some persons have this ability). However I had read Lady
Susan's account closely and nearly committed it to memory, so
the reader can be assured that my version is authoritative.

Letter 12

Sir Reginald De Courcy to his Son.
Parklands.

I know that young Men in general do not admit of any inquiry even from their nearest relations into affairs of the heart, but I hope, my dear Reginald, that you will be superior to such as allow nothing for a Father's anxiety, & think themselves privileged to refuse him their confidence & slight his advice. You must be sensible that as an only son, & the representative of an ancient Family, your conduct in Life is most interesting to your connections. In the very important concern of Marriage especially, there is everything at stake—your own happiness, that of your Parents, & the credit of your name. I do not suppose that you would deliberately form an absolute engagement of that nature without acquainting your Mother & myself, or at least without being convinced that we should approve of your choice; but I cannot help fearing that you may be drawn in, by the Lady who has lately attached you, to a Marriage which the whole of your Family, far & near, must highly reprobate.

Lady Susan's age is itself a material objection, but her want of character is one so much more serious that the difference of even twelve years becomes in comparison of small amount. Were you not blinded by a sort of fascination, it would be ridiculous in me to repeat the instances of great misconduct on her side, so very generally known. Her neglect of her husband, her encouragement of other Men, her extravagance & dissipation, were so gross & notorious that no one could be ignorant of them at the time, nor can now have forgotten them.

To our Family she has always been represented in softened colours by the benevolence of Mr. Charles Vernon; & yet, in spite of his generous endeavours to excuse her, we know that she did, from the most selfish motives, take all possible pains to prevent his marrying Catherine.

My Years & increasing Infirmities make me very desirous, my dear Reginald, of seeing you settled in the world. To the Fortune of your wife, the goodness of my own will make me indifferent; but her family & character must be equally unexceptionable. When your choice is so fixed as that no objection can be made to either, I can promise you a ready & chearful consent; but it is my Duty to oppose a Match which deep Art only could render probable, & must in the end make wretched.

It is possible her behaviour may arise only from Vanity, or the wish of gaining the admiration of a Man whom she must imagine to be particularly prejudiced against her; but it is more likely that she should aim at something farther. She is poor, & may naturally seek an alliance which may be advantageous to herself. You know your own rights, & that it is out of my power to prevent your inheriting the family Estate. My Ability of distressing you during my Life would be a species of revenge to which I should hardly stoop under any circumstances. I honestly tell you my Sentiments & Intentions: I do not wish to work on your Fears, but on your Sense & Affection. It would destroy every comfort of my Life to know that you were married to Lady Susan Vernon: it would be the death of that honest Pride with which I have hitherto considered my son; I should blush to see him, to hear of him, to think of him.

I may perhaps do no good but that of relieving my own mind by this Letter, but I felt it my Duty to tell you that your partiality for Lady Susan is no secret to your friends, & to warn you against her. I should be glad to hear your reasons for disbelieving Mr. Smith's intelligence; you had no doubt of its authenticity a month ago.

If you can give me your assurance of having no design beyond enjoying the conversation of a clever woman for a short period, & of yielding admiration only to her Beauty & Abilities, without being blinded by them to her faults, you will restore me to happiness; but if you cannot do this, explain to me, at least, what has occasioned so great an alteration in your opinion of her.

I am, &c.

REGD. DE COURCY.

Note on Letter the Twelfth: *If more evidence of this account's falseness were needed—which I do not think it is—the actual difference between Reginald's and Lady Susan's ages was thirteen years, not "twelve" as the anonymous Lady has it here.*

Letter 13

Lady De Courcy to Mrs. Vernon.
Parklands.

My dear Catherine

Unluckily I was confined to my room when your last letter came, by a cold which affected my eyes so much as to prevent my reading it myself; so I could not refuse your Father when he offered to read it to me, by which means he became acquainted, to my great vexation, with all your fears about your Brother. I had intended to write to Reginald myself as soon as my eyes would let me, to point out as well as I could the danger of an intimate acquaintance with so artful a woman as Lady Susan, to a young Man of his age & high expectations. I meant, moreover, to have reminded him of our being quite alone now, & very much in need of him to keep up our spirits these long winter evenings. Whether it would have done any good can never be settled now, but I am excessively vexed that Sir Reginald should know anything of a matter which we foresaw would make him so uneasy. He caught all your fears the moment he had read your Letter, and I am sure has not had the business out of his head since. He wrote by the same post to Reginald a long letter full of it all, & particularly asking an explanation of what he may have heard from Lady Susan to contradict the late shocking reports. His answer came this morning, which I shall enclose to you, as I think you will like to see it. I wish it was more satisfactory; but it seems written with such a determination to think well of Lady Susan, that his assurances as to Marriage, &c., do not set my heart at ease. I say all I can, however, to satisfy your Father, & he is certainly less uneasy since Reginald's letter. How provoking it is, my dear Catherine, that this unwelcome Guest of yours should not only prevent our meeting this Christmas, but be the occasion of so much vexation & trouble! Kiss the dear Children for me.

Your affec: Mother,
C. DE COURCY.

Note on Letter the Thirteenth: *"Vexation & trouble!" Who is causing what to whom?*

Letter 14

Mr. De Courcy to Sir Reginald.
Churchill.

My dear Sir

I have this moment received your Letter, which has given me more astonishment than I ever felt before. I am to thank my Sister, I suppose, for having represented me in such a light as to injure me in your opinion, & give you all this alarm. I know not why she should chuse to make herself & her family uneasy by apprehending an Event which no one but herself, I can affirm, would ever have thought possible. To impute such a design to Lady Susan would be taking from her every claim to that excellent understanding which her bitterest Enemies have never denied her; & equally low must sink my pretensions to common sense if I am suspected of matrimonial views in my behaviour to her. Our difference of age must be an insuperable objection, & I entreat you, my dear Sir, to quiet your mind, & no longer harbour a suspicion which cannot be more injurious to your own peace than to our Understandings.

I can have no other view in remaining with Lady Susan, than to enjoy for a short time (as you have yourself expressed it) the conversation of a Woman of high mental powers. If Mrs. Vernon would allow something to my affection for herself & her husband in the length of my visit, she would do more justice to us all; but my Sister is unhappily prejudiced beyond the hope of conviction against Lady Susan. From an attachment to her husband, which in itself does honour to both, she cannot forgive the endeavours at preventing their union which have been attributed to selfishness in Lady Susan; but in this case, as well as in many others, the World has most grossly injured that Lady, by supposing the worst where the motives of her conduct have been doubtful.

Lady Susan had heard something so materially to the disadvantage of my Sister, as to persuade her that the happiness of Mr. Vernon, to whom she was always much attached, would be absolutely destroyed by the Marriage. And this circumstance, while it explains the true motive of Lady Susan's conduct, & removes all the blame which has been so lavished on her, may also convince us how little the general report of any one ought to be credited; since no character, however upright, can escape the malevolence of slander. If my Sister, in the security of retirement, with as little opportunity as inclination to do Evil, could not avoid Censure, we must not rashly condemn those who, living in the World & surrounded with temptation, should be accused of Errors which they are known to have the power of committing.

I blame myself severely for having so easily believed the slanderous tales invented by Charles Smith to the prejudice of Lady Susan, as I am now convinced how greatly they have traduced her. As to Mrs. Manwaring's jealousy, it was totally his own invention, & his account of her attaching Miss Manwaring's Lover was scarcely better founded. Sir James Martin had been drawn in by that young Lady to pay her some attention; & as he is a Man of fortune, it was easy to see that _her_ views extended to Marriage. It is well known that Miss Manwaring is absolutely on the catch for a husband, & no one therefore can pity her for losing, by the superior attractions of another woman, the chance of being able to make a worthy Man completely miserable. Lady Susan was far from intending such a conquest, & on finding how warmly Miss Manwaring resented her Lover's defection, determined, in spite of Mr. & Mrs. Manwaring's most earnest entreaties, to leave the family.

I have reason to imagine that she did receive serious Proposals from Sir James, but her removing to Langford immediately on the discovery of his attachment, must acquit her on that article with any Mind of common candour. You will, I am sure, my dear Sir, feel the truth of this, & will hereby learn to do justice to the character of a very injured Woman.

I know that Lady Susan in coming to Churchill was governed only by the most honourable & amiable intentions; her prudence & economy are exemplary, her regard for Mr. Vernon equal even to _his_ deserts; & her wish of obtaining my sister's good opinion merits a better return than it has received. As a Mother she is unexceptionable; her solid affection for her Child is shewn by placing her in hands where her Education

will be properly attended to; but because she has not
the blind & weak partiality of most Mothers, she is
accused of wanting Maternal Tenderness. Every person
of Sense, however, will know how to value & commend her well-directed affection, & will join me in
wishing that Frederica Vernon may prove more worthy than she has yet done of her Mother's tender care.

I have now, my dear Sir, written my real sentiments
of Lady Susan; you will know from this Letter how
highly I admire her Abilities, & esteem her Character;
but if you are not equally convinced by my full & solemn
assurance that your fears have been most idly created,
you will deeply mortify & distress me.—I am, &c.

R. DE COURCY.

Note on Letter the Fourteenth: *Finally an acknowledg-
ment of the Truth! Curious to find it here—and to divine
what the Lady author's ulterior intention might have been.*

Letter 15

Mrs. Vernon to Lady De Courcy.
Churchill.

My dear Mother

I return you Reginald's letter, & rejoice with all my heart that my Father is made easy by it. Tell him so, with my congratulations; but between ourselves, I must own it has only convinced _me_ of my Brother's having no _present_ intention of marrying Lady Susan—not that he is in no danger of doing so three months hence. He gives a very plausible account of her behaviour at Langford; I wish it may be true, but his intelligence must come from herself, & I am less disposed to believe it than to lament the degree of intimacy subsisting between them implied by the discussion of such a subject.

I am sorry to have incurred his displeasure, but can expect nothing better while he is so very eager in Lady Susan's justification. He is very severe against me indeed, & yet I hope I have not been hasty in my judgement of her. Poor Woman! tho' I have reasons enough for my dislike, I cannot help pitying her at present, as she is in real distress, & with too much cause. She had this morning a letter from the Lady with whom she has placed her daughter, to request that Miss Vernon might be immediately removed, as she had been detected in an attempt to run away. Why, or whither she intended to go, does not appear; but as her situation seems to have been unexceptionable, it is a sad thing, & of course highly afflicting to Lady Susan.

Frederica must be as much as sixteen, & ought to know better; but from what her Mother insinuates, I am afraid she is a perverse girl. She has been sadly neglected, however, & her Mother ought to remember it.

Mr. Vernon set off for Town as soon as she had determined what should be done. He is, if possible, to prevail on Miss Summers to let Frederica continue with her; & if he cannot succeed, to bring her to Churchill for the present, till some other situation can be found for her. Her Ladyship is comforting herself meanwhile by strolling along the Shrubbery with Reginald, calling forth all his tender feelings, I suppose, on this distressing occasion. She has been talking a great deal about it to me. She talks vastly well; I am afraid of being ungenerous, or I should say _too_ well to feel so very deeply. But I will not look for Faults; she may be Reginald's Wife— Heaven forbid it!—but why should I be quicker-sighted than anybody else? Mr. Vernon declares that he never saw deeper distress than hers, on the receipt of the Letter—& is his judgement inferior to mine?

She was very unwilling that Frederica should be allowed to come to Churchill, & justly enough, as it seems a sort of reward to Behaviour deserving very differently; but it was impossible to take her anywhere else, & she is not to remain here long. "It will be absolutely necessary," said she, "as you, my dear Sister, must be sensible, to treat my daughter with some severity while she is here;—a most painful necessity, but I will endeavour to submit to it. I am afraid I have often been too indulgent, but my poor Frederica's temper could never bear opposition well. You must support & encourage me—You must urge the necessity of reproof if you see me too lenient."

All this sounds very reasonably. Reginald is so incensed against the poor silly Girl! Surely it is not to Lady Susan's credit that he should be so bitter against her daughter; his idea of her must be drawn from the Mother's description.

Well, whatever may be his fate, we have the comfort of knowing that we have done our utmost to save him. We must commit the event to an Higher Power. Yours Ever, &c.

CATH. VERNON.

Note on Letter the Fifteenth: *I am not certain that I am in perfect accord with Mr. John Murray's decision to include the authoress' false account as an appendix to this memoir.*

Mr. Murray's reasoning, so far as I follow it, is that the spinster's slanders had already been so widely circulated that they could not do further harm, while directly juxtaposing her malicious inventions with the true account would more clearly and directly refute them.

I cannot forget the troubling factum that Mr. Murray is also the publisher of this Lady's final so-called "novels." Could his true interest be to attract Readers to these other works by attaching her history to a superior volume? Such a conflict of motives is not unknown in the world of book-jobbers, though I make no accusation.

I have therefore decided to refrain further comment on these letters, the malicious falseness of which should be self-evident. Perhaps in future printings—many are anticipated—this slanderous addendum could be omitted, which might permit a lower price, putting a valuable work in the hands of a wider readership.

Letter 16

Lady Susan to Mrs. Johnson.
Churchill.

Never, my dearest Alicia, was I so provoked in my life as by a Letter this morning from Miss Summers. That horrid girl of mine has been trying to run away. I had not a notion of her being such a little devil before, she seemed to have all the Vernon Milkiness; but on receiving the letter in which I declared my intention about Sir James, she actually attempted to elope; at least, I cannot otherwise account for her doing it. She meant, I suppose, to go to the Clarkes in Staffordshire, for she has no other acquaintance. But she _shall_ be punished, she _shall_ have him. I have sent Charles to Town to make matters up if he can, for I do not by any means want her here. If Miss Summers will not keep her, you must find me out another school, unless we can get her married immediately. Miss S. writes word that she could not get the young Lady to assign any cause for her extraordinary conduct, which confirms me in my own private explanation of it. Frederica is too shy, I think, & too much in awe of me to tell tales; but if the mildness of her Uncle _should_ get anything from her, I am not afraid. I trust I shall be able to make my story as good as hers. If I am vain of anything, it is of my eloquence. Consideration & Esteem as surely follow command of Language, as Admiration waits on Beauty. And here I have opportunity enough for the exercise of my Talent, as the cheif of my time is spent in Conversation. Reginald is never easy unless we are by ourselves, & when the weather is tolerable, we pace the shrubbery for hours together. I like him on the whole very well; he is clever & has a good deal to say, but he is sometimes impertinent & troublesome. There is a sort of ridiculous delicacy about him which requires the fullest explanation of whatever he may have heard to my disadvantage, & is never satisfied till he thinks he has ascertained the beginning & end of everything.

This is _one_ sort of Love, but I confess it does not particularly recommend itself to me. I infinitely prefer the tender & liberal spirit of Manwaring, which, impressed with the deepest conviction of my merit, is satisfied that whatever I do must be right; & look with a degree of contempt on the inquisitive & doubtful Fancies of that Heart which seems always debating on the reasonableness of its Emotions. Manwaring is indeed, beyond compare, superior to Reginald—superior in everything but the power of being with me! Poor fellow! he is quite distracted by Jealousy, which I am not sorry for, as I know no better support of Love. He has been teizing me to allow of his coming into this country, & lodging somewhere near _incog._ —but I forbid anything of the kind. Those women are inexcusable who forget what is due to themselves & the opinion of the World.

S. VERNON.

Letter 17

Mrs. Vernon to Lady De Courcy.
Churchill.

My dear Mother

Mr. Vernon returned on Thursday night, bringing his neice with him. Lady Susan had received a line from him by that day's post, informing her that Miss Summers had absolutely refused to allow of Miss Vernon's continuance in her Academy; we were therefore prepared for her arrival, & expected them impatiently the whole evening. They came while we were at Tea, & I never saw any creature look so frightened in my life as Frederica when she entered the room.

Lady Susan, who had been shedding tears before, & shewing great agitation at the idea of the meeting, received her with perfect self-command, & without betraying the least tenderness of spirit. She hardly spoke to her, & on Frederica's bursting into tears as soon as we were seated, took her out of the room, & did not return for some time.

When she did, her eyes looked very red, & she was as much agitated as before. We saw no more of her daughter. Poor Reginald was beyond measure concerned to see his fair friend in such distress, & watched her with so much tender solicitude, that I, who occasionally caught her observing his countenance with exultation, was quite out of patience. This pathetic representation lasted the whole evening, & so ostentatious & artful a display had entirely convinced me that she did in fact feel nothing.

I am more angry with her than ever since I have seen her daughter; the poor girl looks so unhappy that my heart aches for her. Lady Susan is surely too severe, for Frederica does not seem to have the sort of temper to make severity necessary. She looks perfectly timid, dejected, & penitent.

She is very pretty, tho' not so handsome as her Mother, nor at all like her. Her complexion is delicate, but neither so fair nor so blooming as Lady Susan's—& she has quite the Vernon cast of countenance, the oval face & mild dark eyes, & there is peculiar sweetness in her look when she speaks either to her Uncle or me, for as we behave kindly to her we have of course engaged her gratitude. Her Mother has insinuated that her temper is untractable, but I never saw a face less indicative of any evil disposition than hers; & from what I now see of the behaviour of each to the other, the invariable severity of Lady Susan & the silent dejection of Frederica, I am led to believe as heretofore that the former has no real Love for her daughter, & has never done her justice or treated her affectionately.

I have not yet been able to have any conversation with my neice; she is shy, & I think I can see that some pains are taken to prevent her being much with me. Nothing satisfactory transpires as to her reason for running away. Her kind-hearted Uncle, you may be sure, was too fearful of distressing her to ask many questions as they travelled. I wish it had been possible for me to fetch her instead of him; I think I should have discovered the truth in the course of a Thirty-mile Journey.

The small Pianoforte' has been removed within these few days, at Lady Susan's request, into her Dressing room, & Frederica spends great part of the day there; _practising_, it is called; but I seldom hear any noise when I pass that way. What she does with herself there, I do not know; there are plenty of books in the room, but it is not every girl who has been running wild the first fifteen years of her life, that can or will read. Poor Creature! the prospect from her window is not very instructive, for that room overlooks the Lawn, you know, with the Shrubbery on one side, where she may see her Mother walking for an hour together in earnest conversation with Reginald. A girl of Frederica's age must be childish indeed, if such things do not strike her. Is it not inexcusable to give such an example to a daughter? Yet Reginald still thinks Lady Susan the best of Mothers—still condemns Frederica as a worthless girl! He is convinced that her attempt to run away proceeded from no justifiable cause, & had no provocation. I am sure I cannot say that it _had_, but while Miss Summers declares that Miss Vernon shewed no signs of Obstinacy or Perverseness during her whole stay in Wigmore Street, till she was detected in this scheme, I cannot so readily credit what Lady Susan has made him & wants to make me believe, that it was merely an impatience of restraint & a desire of escaping from the tuition of Masters which brought on the plan of an elopement. Oh! Reginald, how is your Judgement enslaved! He scarcely dares even allow her to be handsome, & when I speak of her beauty, replies only that her eyes have no Brilliancy!

Sometimes he is sure she is deficient in Understanding, & at others that her temper only is in fault. In short, when a person is always to deceive, it is impossible to be consistent. Lady Susan finds it necessary for her own justification that Frederica should be to blame, & probably has sometimes judged it expedient to accuse her of ill-nature & sometimes to lament her want of sense. Reginald is only repeating after her Ladyship.

I am &c.
CATH. VERNON.

Letter 18

From the same to the same.
Churchill.

My dear Madam

I am very glad to find that my description of Frederica Vernon has interested you, for I do believe her truly deserving of your regard; & when I have communicated a notion which has recently struck me, your kind impressions in her favour will, I am sure, be heightened. I cannot help fancying that she is growing partial to my Brother; I so very often see her eyes fixed on his face with a remarkable expression of pensive admiration! He is certainly very handsome; & yet more, there is an openness in his manner that must be highly prepossessing, & I am sure she feels it so. Thoughtful & pensive in general, her countenance always brightens into a smile when Reginald says anything amusing; and, let the subject be ever so serious that he may be conversing on, I am much mistaken if a syllable of his uttering escapes her.

I want to make _him_ sensible of all this, for we know the power of gratitude on such a heart as his; & could Frederica's artless affection detach him from her Mother, we might bless the day which brought her to Churchill. I think, my dear Madam, you would not disapprove of her as a Daughter. She is extremely young, to be sure, has had a wretched Education, & a dreadful example of Levity in her Mother; but yet I can pronounce her disposition to be excellent, & her natural abilities very good. Though totally without accomplishments, she is by no means so ignorant as one might expect to find her, being fond of books & spending the cheif of her time in reading. Her Mother leaves her more to herself now than she _did_, & I have her with me as much as possible, & have taken great pains to overcome her timidity. We are very good friends, & tho' she never opens her lips before her Mother, she talks enough when alone with me to make it clear that, if properly treated by Lady Susan, she would always appear to much greater advantage. There cannot be a more gentle, affectionate heart; or more obliging manners, when acting without restraint. Her little Cousins are all very fond of her.

Yrs. affec:ly,

CATH. VERNON.

Letter 19

Lady Susan to Mrs. Johnson.
Churchill.

You will be eager, I know, to hear something farther of Frederica, & perhaps may think me negligent for not writing before. She arrived with her Uncle last Thursday fortnight, when, of course, I lost no time in demanding the reason of her behaviour; & soon found myself to have been perfectly right in attributing it to my own letter. The purport of it frightened her so thoroughly that, with a mixture of true girlish perverseness & folly, without considering that she could not escape from my authority by running away from Wigmore Street, she resolved on getting out of the house & proceeding directly by the stage to her friends, the Clarkes; & had really got as far as the length of two streets in her journey when she was fortunately miss'd, pursued, & overtaken.

Such was the first distinguished exploit of Miss Frederica Susanna Vernon; & if we consider that it was achieved at the tender age of sixteen, we shall have room for the most flattering prognostics of her future renown. I am excessively provoked, however, at the parade of propriety which prevented Miss Summers from keeping the girl; & it seems so extraordinary a piece of nicety, considering my daughter's family connections, that I can only suppose the Lady to be governed by the fear of never getting her money. Be that as it may, however, Frederica is returned on my hands; and having now nothing else to employ her, is busy in pursuing the plan of Romance begun at Langford. She is actually falling in love with Reginald De Courcy! To disobey her Mother by refusing an unexceptionable offer is not enough; her affections must likewise be given without her Mother's approbation. I never saw a girl of her age bid fairer to be the sport of Mankind. Her feelings are tolerably acute, & she is so charmingly artless in their display as to afford the most reasonable hope of her being ridiculed & despised by every Man who sees her.

Artlessness will never do in Love matters; & that girl is born a simpleton who has it either by nature or affectation. I am not yet certain that Reginald sees what she is about; nor is it of much consequence. She is now an object of indifference to him; she would be one of contempt were he to understand her Emotions. Her beauty is much admired by the Vernons, but it has no effect on _him_. She is in high favour with her Aunt altogether—because she is so little like myself, of course. She is exactly the companion for Mrs. Vernon, who dearly loves to be first, & to have all the sense & all the wit of the Conversation to herself: Frederica

Letter 20

Mrs. Vernon to Lady De Courcy.
Churchill.

We have a very unexpected Guest with us at present, my
dear Mother. He arrived yesterday. I heard a carriage at
the door, as I was sitting with my children while they
dined; & supposing I should be wanted, left the Nursery
soon afterwards, & was half-way downstairs, when Frederica, as pale as ashes, came running up, & rushed by me
into her own room. I instantly followed, & asked her
what was the matter. "Oh!" cried she, "he is come, Sir
James is come—& what am I to do?" This was no explanation; I begged her to tell me what she meant. At that
moment we were interrupted by a knock at the door: it
was Reginald, who came, by Lady Susan's direction, to
call Frederica down. "It is Mr. De Courcy!" said she,
colouring violently. "Mamma has sent for me, & I must
go." We all three went down together; & I saw my
Brother examining the terrified face of Frederica with
surprise. In the breakfast-room we found Lady Susan, & a
young Man of genteel appearance, whom she introduced

to me by the name of Sir James Martin—the very person, as you may remember, whom it was said she had been at pains to detach from Miss Manwaring. But the conquest, it seems, was not designed for herself, or she has since transferred it to her daughter; for Sir James is now desperately in love with Frederica, & with full encouragement from Mama. The poor girl, however, I am sure, dislikes him; & tho' his person & address are very well, he appears, both to Mr. Vernon & me, a very weak young Man.

Frederica looked so shy, so confused, when we entered the room, that I felt for her exceedingly. Lady Susan behaved with great attention to her Visitor; & yet I thought I could perceive that she had no particular pleasure in seeing him. Sir James talked a great deal, & made many civil excuses to me for the liberty he had taken in coming to Churchill—mixing more frequent laughter with his discourse than the subject required—said many things over & over again, & told Lady Susan three times that he had seen Mrs. Johnson a few Evenings before. He now & then addressed Frederica, but more frequently her Mother. The poor girl sat all this time without opening her lips—her eyes cast down, & her colour varying every instant; while Reginald observed all that passed in perfect silence.

At length Lady Susan, weary I believe of her situation, proposed walking; & we left the two gentlemen together, to put on our Pelisses.

As we went upstairs, Lady Susan begged permission to attend me for a few moments in my Dressing room, as she was anxious to speak with me in private. I led her thither accordingly, & as soon as the door was closed, she said, "I was never more surprised in my life than by Sir James's arrival, & the suddenness of it requires some apology to _You_, my dear Sister; tho' to _me_, as a Mother, it is highly flattering. He is so extremely attached to my Daughter that he could not exist longer without seeing her. Sir James is a young man of an amiable disposition & excellent character; a little too much of the _Rattle_, perhaps, but a year or two will rectify _that_; & he is in other respects so very eligible a Match for Frederica, that I have always observed his attachment with the greatest pleasure, & am persuaded that you & my Brother will give the alliance your hearty approbation. I have never before mentioned the likelihood of its taking place to any one, because I thought that while Frederica continued at school it had better not be known to exist; but now, as I am convinced that Frederica is too old ever to submit to school confinement, & have therefore begun to consider her union with Sir James as not very distant, I had intended within a few days to acquaint yourself & Mr. Vernon with the whole business. I am sure, my dear Sister, you will excuse my remaining silent so long, & agree with me that such circumstances, while they continue from any cause in suspense, cannot be too cautiously concealed. When you have the happiness of bestowing your sweet little Catherine, some years hence, on a Man who in connection & character is alike unexceptionable, you will know what I feel now; tho' Thank Heaven! you cannot have all my reasons for rejoicing in such an Event. Catherine will be amply provided for, & not, like my Frederica, indebted to a fortunate Establishment

for the comforts of Life." She concluded by demanding
my congratulations. I gave them somewhat awkwardly,
I believe; for in fact, the sudden disclosure of so important a matter took from me the power of speaking with
any clearness. She thanked me, however, most affectionately, for my kind concern in the welfare of herself
& daughter; & then said, "I am not apt to deal in professions, my dear Mrs. Vernon, & I never had the convenient talent of affecting sensations foreign to my heart;
& therefore I trust you will believe me when I declare
that, much as I had heard in your praise before I knew
you, I had no idea that I should ever love you as I now
do; & I must further say that your friendship towards
me is more particularly gratifying because I have reason
to believe that some attempts were made to prejudice
you against me. I only wish that They—whoever they
are—to whom I am indebted for such kind intentions,
could see the terms on which we now are together, &
understand the real affection we feel for each other! But
I will not detain you any longer. God bless you for your
goodness to me & my girl, & continue to you all your
present happiness." What can one say of such a Woman,
my dear Mother? Such earnestness, such solemnity of
expression! & yet I cannot help suspecting the truth of
everything she said.

As for Reginald, I believe he does not know what
to make of the matter. When Sir James first came, he
appeared all astonishment & perplexity. The folly of
the young Man & the confusion of Frederica entirely
engrossed him; & tho' a little private discourse with
Lady Susan has since had its effect, he is still hurt, I am

sure, at her allowing of such a Man's attentions to her daughter.

Sir James invited himself with great composure to remain here a few days—hoped we would not think it odd, was aware of its being very impertinent, but he took the liberty of a relation; & concluded by wishing, with a laugh, that he might be really one soon. Even Lady Susan seemed a little disconcerted by this forwardness; in her heart, I am persuaded, she sincerely wishes him gone.

But something must be done for this poor Girl, if her feelings are such as both her Uncle & I believe them to be. She must not be sacrificed to Policy or Ambition; she must not be even left to suffer from the dread of it. The Girl whose heart can distinguish Reginald De Courcy deserves, however he may slight her, a better fate than to be Sir James Martin's wife. As soon as I can get her alone, I will discover the real Truth; but she seems to wish to avoid me. I hope this does not proceed from anything wrong, & that I shall not find out I have thought too well of her. Her behaviour to Sir James certainly speaks the greatest consciousness & Embarrassment, but I see nothing in it more like Encouragement. Adieu, my dear Madam.

Yrs, &c.

CATH. VERNON.

Dear Mr. Murray, I would urge you to reconsider your intention of publishing this Lady's account as an appendix to mine. It is not only false, it is malicious and—dare I say?—vulgar. As such its publication can do little credit to your esteemed firm. I remain, yours faithfully, Rufus Martin-Colonna

Letter 21

Miss Vernon to Mr. De Courcy.

Sir,

I hope you will excuse this liberty; I am forced upon it by the greatest distress, or I should be ashamed to trouble you. I am very miserable about Sir James Martin, & have no other way in the world of helping myself but by writing to you, for I am forbidden ever speaking to my Uncle or Aunt on the subject; & this being the case, I am afraid my applying to you will appear no better than equivocation, & as if I attended only to the letter & not the spirit of Mama's commands. But if _you_ do not take my part & persuade her to break it off, I shall be half distracted, for I cannot bear him. No human Being but _you_ could have any chance of prevailing with her. If you will, therefore, have the unspeakable great kindness of taking my part with her, & persuading her to send Sir James away, I shall be more obliged to you than it is possible for me to express. I always disliked him from the first; it is not a sudden fancy, I

assure you, Sir; I always thought him silly & impertinent & disagreable, & now he is grown worse than
ever. I would rather work for my bread than marry
him. I do not know how to apologize enough for this
Letter; I know it is taking so great a liberty; I am aware
how dreadfully angry it will make Mama, but I must
run the risk. I am, Sir, your most Humble Servt.

F. S. V.

Letter 22

Lady Susan to Mrs. Johnson.
Churchill.

This is insufferable! My dearest friend, I was never so
enraged before, & must relieve myself by writing to
you, who I know will enter into all my feelings. Who
should come on Tuesday but Sir James Martin! Guess
my astonishment & vexation—for, as you well know, I
never wished him to be seen at Churchill. What a pity
that you should not have known his intentions! Not
content with coming, he actually invited himself to
remain here a few days. I could have poisoned him! I
made the best of it, however, & told my story with great
success to Mrs. Vernon, who, whatever might be her
real sentiments, said nothing in opposition to mine. I
made a point also of Frederica's behaving civilly to Sir
James, & gave her to understand that I was absolutely
determined on her marrying him. She said something
of her misery, but that was all. I have for some time
been more particularly resolved on the Match from seeing the rapid increase of her affection for Reginald, &

from not feeling perfectly secure that a knowledge of _ that_ affection might not in the end awaken a return. Contemptible as a regard founded only on compassion must make them both in my eyes, I felt by no means assured that such might not be the consequence. It is true that Reginald had not in any degree grown cool towards me; but yet he had lately mentioned Frederica spontaneously & unnecessarily, & once had said something in praise of her person. _He_ was all astonishment at the appearance of my visitor, & at first observed Sir James with an attention which I was pleased to see not unmixed with jealousy; but unluckily it was impossible for me really to torment him, as Sir James, tho' extremely gallant to me, very soon made the whole party understand that his heart was devoted to my daughter.

I had no great difficulty in convincing De Courcy, when we were alone, that I was perfectly justified, all things considered, in desiring the match; & the whole business seemed most comfortably arranged. They could none of them help perceiving that Sir James was no Solomon; but I had positively forbidden Frederica's complaining to Charles Vernon or his wife, & they had therefore no pretence for Interference; tho' my impertinent Sister, I believe, wanted only opportunity for doing so.

Everything, however, was going on calmly & quietly; & tho' I counted the hours of Sir James's stay, my mind was entirely satisfied with the posture of affairs. Guess, then, what I must feel at the sudden disturbance of all my schemes; & that, too, from a quarter whence I had least reason to apprehend it. Reginald came this

morning into my Dressing room with a very unusual
solemnity of countenance, & after some preface
informed me in so many words that he wished to reason with me on the Impropriety & Unkindness of
allowing Sir James Martin to address my Daughter
contrary to _her_ inclination. I was all amazement.
When I found that he was not to be laughed out of his
design, I calmly required an explanation, & begged to
know by what he was impelled, & by whom commissioned to reprimand me. He then told me, mixing in
his speech a few insolent compliments, & ill-timed
expressions of Tenderness, to which I listened with
perfect indifference, that my daughter had acquainted
him with some circumstances concerning herself, Sir
James, & me, which gave him great uneasiness.

In short, I found that she had in the first place actually written to him to request his interference, & that
on receiving her Letter, he had conversed with her on
the subject of it, in order to understand the particulars,
& assure himself of her real wishes!

I have not a doubt but that the girl took this opportunity of making downright Love to him. I am convinced of it from the manner in which he spoke of her.
Much good may such Love do him! I shall ever despise
the Man who can be gratified by the Passion which he
never wished to inspire, nor solicited the avowal of. I
shall always detest them both. He can have no true
regard for me, or he would not have listened to her; and
she, with her little rebellious heart & indelicate feelings,
to throw herself into the protection of a young Man
with whom she has scarcely ever exchanged two words

before! I am equally confounded at _her_ Impudence &
his Credulity. How dared he believe what she told
him in my disfavour! Ought he not to have felt assured
that I must have unanswerable Motives for all that I had
done? Where was his reliance on my Sense & Goodness
then? Where the resentment which true Love would
have dictated against the person defaming me—that
person, too, a Chit, a Child, without Talent or Education, whom he had been always taught to despise?

I was calm for some time; but the greatest degree of
Forbearance may be overcome, & I hope I was afterwards sufficiently keen. He endeavoured, long endeavoured, to soften my resentment; but that woman is a
fool indeed who, while insulted by accusation, can be
worked on by compliments. At length he left me, as
deeply provoked as myself; & he shewed his anger
more. I was quite cool, but he gave way to the most
violent indignation. I may therefore expect it will the
sooner subside; & perhaps his may be vanished forever,
while mine will be found still fresh & implacable.

He is now shut up in his apartment, whither I heard
him go on leaving mine. How unpleasant, one would
think, must his reflections be! But some people's feelings are incomprehensible. I have not yet tranquillized
myself enough to see Frederica. _She_ shall not soon
forget the occurrences of this day; she shall find that
she has poured forth her tender Tale of Love in vain, &
exposed herself forever to the contempt of the whole
world, & the severest Resentment of her injured Mother.

Yrs. affec:ly

S. VERNON.

Letter 23

Mrs. Vernon to Lady De Courcy.
Churchill.

Let me congratulate you, my dearest Mother! The affair which has given us so much anxiety is drawing to a happy conclusion. Our prospect is most delightful; & since matters have now taken so favourable a turn, I am quite sorry that I ever imparted my apprehensions to you; for the pleasure of learning that the danger is over is perhaps dearly purchased by all that you have previously suffered.

I am so much agitated by Delight that I can scarcely hold a pen; but am determined to send you a few short lines by James, that you may have some explanation of what must so greatly astonish you, as that Reginald should be returning to Parklands.

I was sitting about half an hour ago with Sir James in the Breakfast parlour, when my Brother called me out of the room. I instantly saw that something was the matter; his complexion was raised, & he spoke with great emotion. You know his eager manner, my dear Madam, when his mind is interested.

"Catherine," said he, "I am going home today; I am sorry to leave you, but I must go. It is a great while since I have seen my Father & Mother. I am going to send James forward with my Hunters immediately; if you have any Letter, therefore, he can take it. I shall not be at home myself till Wednesday or Thursday, as I shall go through London, where I have business. But before I leave you," he continued, speaking in a lower voice, & with still greater energy, "I must warn you of one thing—do not let Frederica Vernon be made unhappy by that Martin. He wants to marry her—her Mother promotes the Match—but _she_ cannot endure the idea of it. Be assured that I speak from the fullest conviction of the Truth of what I say; I _know_ that Frederica is made wretched by Sir James' continuing here. She is a sweet girl, & deserves a better fate. Send him away immediately. _He_ is only a fool—but what her Mother can mean, Heaven only knows! Good-bye," he added, shaking my hand with earnestness—"I do not know when you will see me again; but remember what I tell you of Frederica; you _must_ make it your business to see justice done her. She is an amiable girl, & has a very superior Mind to what we have ever given her credit for."

He then left me, & ran upstairs. I would not try to stop him, for I know what his feelings must be; the nature of mine, as I listened to him, I need not attempt to describe. For a minute or two, I remained in the same spot, overpowered by wonder—of a most agreable sort indeed; yet it required some consideration to be tranquilly happy.

In about ten minutes after my return to the parlour, Lady Susan entered the room. I concluded, of course, that she & Reginald had been quarrelling, & looked with anxious curiosity for a confirmation of my beleif in her face. Mistress of Deceit, however, she appeared perfectly unconcerned, & after chatting on indifferent subjects for a short time, said to me, "I find from Wilson that we are going to lose Mr. De Courcy—is it true that he leaves Churchill this morning?" I replied that it was. "He told us nothing of all this last night," said she, laughing, "or even this morning at Breakfast; but perhaps he did not know it himself. Young Men are often hasty in their resolutions—& not more sudden in forming than unsteady in keeping them. I should not be surprised if he were to change his mind at last, & not go." She soon afterwards left the room. I trust, however, my dear Mother, that we have no reason to fear an alteration of his present plan; things have gone too far. They must have quarrelled, & about Frederica too. Her calmness astonishes me. What delight will be yours in seeing him again, in seeing him still worthy of your Esteem, still capable of forming your Happiness!

When I next write, I shall be able, I hope, to tell you that Sir James is gone, Lady Susan vanquished, & Frederica at peace. We have much to do, but it shall be done. I am all impatience to hear how this astonishing change was effected. I finish as I began, with the warmest congratulations.

Yrs. Ever,

CATH. VERNON.

Letter 24

From the same to the same.
Churchill.

Little did I imagine, my dear Mother, when I sent off
my last letter, that the delightful perturbation of spirits
I was then in would undergo so speedy, so melancholy
a reverse! I never can sufficiently regret that I wrote to
you at all. Yet who could have foreseen what has happened? My dear Mother, every hope which but two
hours ago made me so happy is vanished. The quarrel
between Lady Susan & Reginald is made up, & we are
all as we were before. One point only is gained; Sir
James Martin is dismissed. What are we now to look
forward to? I am indeed disappointed. Reginald was all
but gone, his horse was ordered & all but brought to
the door! Who would not have felt safe?

For half an hour, I was in momentary expectation
of his departure. After I had sent off my Letter to you, I
went to Mr. Vernon, & sat with him in his room talking
over the whole matter. I then determined to look for
Frederica, whom I had not seen since breakfast. I met

her on the stairs, & saw that she was crying. "My dear
Aunt," said she, "he is going—Mr. De Courcy is going,
& it is all my fault. I am afraid you will be angry, but
indeed I had no idea it would end so."

"My Love," replied I, "do not think it necessary to
apologize to me on that account. I shall feel myself under
an obligation to any one who is the means of sending
my brother home, because," recollecting myself, "I
know my Father wants very much to see him. But what
is it that _you_ have done to occasion all this?"

She blushed deeply as she answered, "I was so
unhappy about Sir James that I could not help—I have
done something very wrong I know—but you have not
an idea of the misery I have been in, & Mama had
ordered me never to speak to you or my Uncle about
it,—&—" "You therefore spoke to my Brother, to
engage _his_ interference," said I, to save her the explanation. "No; but I wrote to him—I did indeed. I got up
this morning before it was light—I was two hours about
it—& when my Letter was done, I thought I never
should have courage to give it. After breakfast, however,
as I was going to my room, I met him in the passage, &
then, as I knew that everything must depend on that
moment, I forced myself to give it. He was so good as to
take it immediately. I dared not look at him, & ran away
directly. I was in such a fright that I could hardly breathe.
My dear Aunt, you do not know how miserable I have
been."

"Frederica," said I, "you ought to have told _me_ all
your distresses. You would have found in me a friend
always ready to assist you. Do you think that your Uncle

& I should not have espoused your cause as warmly as my Brother?"

"Indeed, I did not doubt your goodness," said she, colouring again, "but I thought Mr. De Courcy could do anything with my Mother; but I was mistaken: they have had a dreadful quarrel about it, & he is going. Mama will never forgive me, & I shall be worse off than ever." "No, you shall not," replied I.—"In such a point as this, your Mother's prohibition ought not to have prevented your speaking to me on the subject. She has no right to make you unhappy, & she shall _not_ do it. Your applying, however, to Reginald can be productive only of Good to all parties. I believe it is best as it is. Depend upon it that you shall not be made unhappy any longer."

At that moment, how great was my astonishment at seeing Reginald come out of Lady Susan's Dressing room. My heart misgave me instantly. His confusion on seeing me was very evident.

Frederica immediately disappeared. "Are you going?" said I. "You will find Mr. Vernon in his own room." "No, Catherine," replied he, "I am _not_ going. Will you let me speak to you a moment?" We went into my room. "I find," continued he, his confusion increasing as he spoke, "that I have been acting with my usual foolish impetuosity. I have entirely misunderstood Lady Susan, & was on the point of leaving the house under a false impression of her conduct. There has been some very great mistake—we have been all mistaken, I fancy. Frederica does not know her Mother—Lady Susan means nothing but her Good—but Frederica will not make a friend of her. Lady Susan therefore does not

always know what will make her daughter happy.
Besides, _I_ could have no right to interfere—Miss Vernon was mistaken in applying to me. In short, Catherine, everything has gone wrong—but it is now all
happily settled. Lady Susan, I believe, wishes to speak to
you about it, if you are at leisure."

"Certainly," replied I, deeply sighing at the recital of
so lame a story. I made no comments, however, for
words would have been vain.

Reginald was glad to get away; & I went to Lady
Susan; curious, indeed, to hear her account of it. "Did I
not tell you," said she, with a smile, "that your Brother
would not leave us after all?" "You did, indeed," replied
I, very gravely; "but I flattered myself that you would be
mistaken." "I should not have hazarded such an opinion," returned she, "if it had not at that moment occurred
to me that his resolution of going might be occasioned
by a Conversation in which we had been this morning
engaged, & which had ended very much to his Dissatis-
faction, from our not rightly understanding each other's
meaning. This idea struck me at the moment, & I
instantly determined that an accidental dispute, in which
I might probably be as much to blame as himself, should
not deprive you of your Brother. If you remember, I left
the room almost immediately. I was resolved to lose no
time in clearing up those mistakes as far as I could. The
case was this: Frederica had set herself violently against
marrying Sir James—" "And can your Ladyship wonder
that she should?" cried I, with some warmth; "Frederica
has an excellent Understanding, & Sir James has none."
"I am at least very far from regretting it, my dear sister,"

said she; "on the contrary, I am grateful for so favourable a sign of my Daughter's sense. Sir James is certainly under par—(his boyish manners make him appear the worse)—& had Frederica possessed the penetration, the abilities which I could have wished in my Daughter, or had I even known her to possess as much as she does, I should not have been anxious for the match." "It is odd that you should alone be ignorant of your Daughter's sense." "Frederica never does justice to herself; her manners are shy & childish. She is besides afraid of me; she scarcely loves me. During her poor Father's life she was a spoilt child; the severity which it has since been necessary for me to shew has alienated her affection; neither has she any of that Brilliancy of Intellect, that Genius, or Vigour of Mind which will force itself forward." "Say rather that she has been unfortunate in her education!" "Heaven knows, my dearest Mrs. Vernon, how fully I am aware of _that_; but I would wish to forget every circumstance that might throw blame on the memory of one whose name is sacred with me."

Here she pretended to cry; I was out of patience with her. "But what," said I, "was your Ladyship going to tell me about your disagreement with my Brother?" "It originated in an action of my Daughter's which equally marks her want of Judgement & the unfortunate Dread of me I have been mentioning—she wrote to Mr. De Courcy." "I know she did; you had forbidden her speaking to Mr. Vernon or to me on the cause of her distress; what could she do, therefore, but apply to my Brother?" "Good God!" she exclaimed, "what an opinion you must have of me! Can you possibly suppose that I was aware of her unhappiness? that it was my object to make my own child miserable, & that I had forbidden her speaking to you on the subject from fear of your interrupting the Diabolical scheme? Do you think me destitute of every honest, every natural feeling? Am I capable of consigning _her_ to everlasting Misery whose welfare it is my first Earthly Duty to promote?" "The idea is horrible. What, then, was your intention when you insisted on her silence?" "Of what use, my dear Sister, could be any application to you, however the affair might stand? Why should I subject you to entreaties which I refused to attend to myself? Neither for your sake, for hers, nor for my own, could such a thing be desirable. When my own resolution was taken, I could not wish for the interference, however friendly, of another person. I was mistaken, it is true, but I believed myself right."

"But what was this mistake to which your Ladyship so often alludes? From whence arose so astonishing a misconception of your Daughter's feelings? Did you not know that she disliked Sir James?" "I knew that he was not absolutely the Man she would have chosen, but I was persuaded that her objections to him did not arise from any perception of his Deficiency. You must not question me, however, my dear Sister, too minutely on this point," continued she, taking me affectionately by the hand; "I honestly own that there is something to conceal. Frederica makes me very unhappy! Her applying to Mr. De Courcy hurt me particularly." "What is it you mean to infer," said I, "by this appearance of mystery? If you think your Daughter at all attached to Reginald, her objecting to Sir James could not less deserve to be attended to than if the cause of her objecting had been a consciousness of his folly; & why should your Ladyship, at any rate, quarrel with my Brother for an interference which you must know it is not in his nature to refuse when urged in such a manner?"

"His disposition, you know, is warm, & he came to expostulate with me; his compassion all alive for this ill-used Girl, this Heroine in distress! We misunderstood each other: he believed me more to blame than I really was; I considered his interference less excusable than I now find it. I have a real regard for him, & was beyond expression mortified to find it, as I thought, so ill bestowed. We were both warm, & of course both to blame. His resolution of leaving Churchill is consistent with his general eagerness. When I understood his intention, however, & at the same time began to think that we had been perhaps equally mistaken in each other's meaning, I resolved to have an explanation before it was too late. For any Member of your Family I must always feel a degree of affection, & I own it would have sensibly hurt me if my acquaintance with Mr. De Courcy had ended so gloomily. I have now only to say farther, that as I am convinced of Frederica's having a reasonable dislike to Sir James, I shall instantly inform him that he must give up all hope of her. I reproach myself for having ever, tho' innocently, made her unhappy on that score. She shall have all the retribution in my power to make; if she value her own happiness as much as I do, if she judge wisely, & command herself as she ought, she may now be easy. Excuse me, my dearest Sister, for thus trespassing on your time, but I owed it to my own Character; & after this explanation I trust I am in no danger of sinking in your opinion."

I could have said, "Not much, indeed!" but I left her almost in silence. It was the greatest stretch of Forbearance I could practise. I could not have stopped myself had I begun. Her assurance, her Deceit—but I will not allow myself to dwell on them; they will strike you sufficiently. My heart sickens within me.

As soon as I was tolerably composed I returned to the Parlour. Sir James's carriage was at the door, & he, merry as usual, soon afterwards took his leave. How easily does her Ladyship encourage or dismiss a Lover!

In spite of this release, Frederica still looks unhappy, still fearful, perhaps, of her Mother's anger; & tho' dreading my Brother's departure, jealous, it may be, of his staying. I see how closely she observes him & Lady Susan. Poor Girl, I have now no hope for her. There is not a chance of her affection being returned. He thinks very differently of her from what he used to do, he does her some justice, but his reconciliation with her Mother precludes every dearer hope.

Prepare, my dear Madam, for the worst. The probability of their marrying is surely heightened. He is more securely hers than ever. When that wretched Event takes place, Frederica must wholly belong to us.

I am thankful that my last Letter will precede this by so little, as every moment that you can be saved from feeling a Joy which leads only to disappointment is of consequence.

Yrs. Ever,
CATH. VERNON.

Letter 25

Lady Susan to Mrs. Johnson.
Churchill.

I call on you, dear Alicia, for congratulations: I am again myself;—gay and triumphant! When I wrote to you the other day I was, in truth, in high irritation, and with ample cause. Nay, I know not whether I ought to be quite tranquil now, for I have had more trouble in restoring peace than I ever intended to submit to—a spirit, too, resulting from a fancied sense of superior Integrity, which is peculiarly insolent! I shall not easily forgive him, I assure you. He was actually on the point of leaving Churchill! I had scarcely concluded my last, when Wilson brought me word of it. I found, therefore, that something must be done; for I did not chuse to leave my character at the mercy of a Man whose passions are so violent and resentful. It would have been trifling with my reputation to allow of his departing with such an impression in my disfavour; in this light, condescension was necessary.

I sent Wilson to say that I desired to speak with him before he went; he came immediately. The angry emotions which had marked every feature when we last parted were partially subdued. He seemed astonished at the summons, & looked as if half wishing & half fearing to be softened by what I might say.

If my Countenance expressed what I aimed at, it was composed and dignified—and yet with a degree of pensiveness which might convince him that I was not quite happy. "I beg your pardon Sir, for the liberty I have taken in sending for you, said I; but as I have just learnt your intention of leaving this place to-day, I feel it my duty to entreat that you will not on my account shorten your visit here even an hour. I am perfectly aware that after what has passed between us it would ill suit the feelings of either to remain longer in the same house: so very great, so total a change from the intimacy of Friendship must render any future intercourse the severest punishment; & your resolution of quitting Churchill is undoubtedly in unison with our situation, & with those lively feelings which I know you to possess. But at the same time it is not for me to suffer such a sacrifice as it must be to leave Relations to whom you are so much attached & are so dear. My remaining here cannot give that pleasure to Mr. & Mrs. Vernon which your society must; & my visit has already perhaps been too long. My removal, therefore, which must at any rate take place soon, may with perfect convenience be hastened; & I make it my particular request that I may not in any way be instrumental in separating a family so affectionately attached to each other. Where _I_ go is of no consequence to any one; of very little to myself; but _you_ are of importance to all your connections." Here I concluded, & I hope you

will be satisfied with my speech. Its effect on Reginald
justifies some portion of vanity, for it was no less favourable than instantaneous. Oh, how delightful it was to
watch the variations of his Countenance while I spoke!
to see the struggle between returning Tenderness & the
remains of Displeasure. There is something agreable in
feelings so easily worked on; not that I envy him their
possession, nor would, for the world, have such myself;
but they are very convenient when one wishes to influence the passions of another. And yet this Reginald,
whom a very few words from me softened at once into
the utmost submission, & rendered more tractable, more
attached, more devoted than ever, would have left me in
the first angry swelling of his proud heart without deigning to seek an explanation.

Humbled as he now is, I cannot forgive him such an
instance of pride, & am doubtful whether I ought not to
punish him by dismissing him at once after this reconciliation, or by marrying & teizing him for ever. But
these measures are each too violent to be adopted without some deliberation; at present my Thoughts are fluc-
tuating between various schemes. I have many things
to compass: I must punish Frederica, & pretty severely
too, for her application to Reginald; I must punish him
for receiving it so favourably, & for the rest of his conduct. I must torment my Sister-in-law for the insolent
triumph of her Look & Manner since Sir James has been
dismissed; for in reconciling Reginald to me, I was not
able to save that ill-fated young Man;—& I must make
myself amends for the humiliation to which I have
stooped within these few days. To effect all this I have

various plans. I have also an idea of being soon in Town; & whatever may be my determination as to the rest, I shall probably put _that_ project in execution—for London will always be the fairest field of action, however my views may be directed; & at any rate I shall there be rewarded by your society, & a little Dissipation, for a ten weeks' penance at Churchill.

I believe I owe it to my own Character to complete the match between my daughter & Sir James, after having so long intended it. Let me know your opinion on this point. Flexibility of Mind, a Disposition easily biassed by others, is an attribute which you know I am not very desirous of obtaining; nor has Frederica any claim to the indulgence of her notions at the expense of her Mother's inclination. Her idle Love for Reginald, too! It is surely my duty to discourage such romantic nonsense. All things considered, therefore, it seems incumbent on me to take her to Town & marry her immediately to Sir James.

When my own will is effected contrary to his, I shall have some credit in being on good terms with Reginald, which at present, in fact, I have not; for tho' he is still in my power, I have given up the very article by which our quarrel was produced, & at best the honour of victory is doubtful.

Send me your opinion on all these matters, my dear Alicia, & let me know whether you can get lodgings to suit me within a short distance of you.

Yr. most attached
S. VERNON.

Letter 26

Mrs. Johnson to Lady Susan.
Edward St.

I am gratified by your reference, & this is my advice: that you come to Town yourself, without loss of time, but that you leave Frederica behind. It would surely be much more to the purpose to get yourself well established by marrying Mr. De Courcy, than to irritate him & the rest of his family by making her marry Sir James. You should think more of yourself & less of your Daughter. She is not of a disposition to do you credit in the World, & seems precisely in her proper place at Churchill, with the Vernons. But _you_ are fitted for Society, & it is shameful to have you exiled from it. Leave Frederica, therefore, to punish herself for the plague she has given you, by indulging that romantic tender-heartedness which will always ensure her misery enough, & come yourself to Town as soon as you can.

I have another reason for urging this:

Manwaring came to town last week, & has contrived, in spite of Mr. Johnson, to make opportunities of seeing me. He is absolutely miserable about you, & jealous to such a degree of De Courcy, that it would be highly unadvisable for them to meet at present. And yet, if you do not allow him to see you here, I cannot answer for his not committing same great imprudence—such as going to Churchill, for instance, which would be dreadful! Besides, if you take my advice, & resolve to marry De Courcy, it will be indispensably necessary to you to get Manwaring out of the way; & you only can have influence enough to send him back to his wife. I have still another motive for your coming: Mr. Johnson leaves London next Tuesday; he is going for his health to Bath, where, if the waters are favourable to his constitution & my wishes, he will be laid up with the gout many weeks. During his absence we shall be able to choose our own society, & to have true enjoyment. I would ask you to Edward Street, but that he once forced from me a kind of promise never to invite you to my house; nothing but my being in the utmost distress for Money should have extorted it from me. I can get you, however, a nice Drawing-room-apartment in Upper Seymour St, & we may be always together there or here; for I consider my promise to Mr. Johnson as comprehending only (at least in his absence) your not sleeping in the House.

Poor Manwaring gives me such histories of his wife's jealousy. Silly Woman, to expect constancy from so charming a Man! but she always was silly—intolerably so in marrying him at all. She the Heiress of a large Fortune, he without a shilling! _One_ title, I know, she might have had, besides Baronets. Her folly in forming the connection was so great that tho' Mr. Johnson was her Guardian, & I do not in general share his feelings, I never can forgive her.

Adieu, Yours, ALICIA.

Letter 27

Mrs. Vernon to Lady De Courcy.
Churchill.

This letter, my dear Mother, will be brought you by Reginald. His long visit is about to be concluded at last, but I fear the separation takes place too late to do us any good. _She_ is going to London to see her particular friend, Mrs. Johnson. It was at first her intention that Frederica should accompany her, for the benefit of Masters, but we over-ruled her there. Frederica was wretched in the idea of going, & I could not bear to have her at the mercy of her Mother; not all the Masters in London could compensate for the ruin of her comfort. I should have feared, too, for her health, & for everything but her Principles—_there_ I believe she is not to be injured by her Mother, or all her Mother's friends; but with those friends (a very bad set, I doubt not) she must have mixed, or have been left in total solitude, & I can hardly tell which would have been worse for her. If she is with her Mother, moreover, she must, alas! in all probability be with Reginald—& that would be the greatest evil of all.

Here we shall in time be in peace. Our regular employments, our Books & conversation, with Exercise, the Children, & every domestic pleasure in my power to procure her, will, I trust, gradually overcome this youthful attachment. I should not have a doubt of it, were she slighted for any other woman in the world than her own Mother.

How long Lady Susan will be in Town, or whether she returns here again, I know not. I could not be cordial in my invitation; but if she chuses to come, no want of cordiality on my part will keep her away.

I could not help asking Reginald if he intended being in Town this winter, as soon as I found her Ladyship's steps would be bent thither; & tho' he professed himself quite undetermined, there was something in his look & voice as he spoke which contradicted his words. I have done with Lamentation. I look upon the event as so far decided that I resign myself to it in despair. If he leaves you soon for London, everything will be concluded.

Your affecly
C. VERNON.

Letter 28

Mrs. Johnson to Lady Susan.
Edward St.

My dearest Friend

I write in the greatest distress; the most unfortunate event has just taken place. Mr. Johnson has hit on the most effectual manner of plaguing us all. He had heard, I imagine, by some means or other, that you were soon to be in London, & immediately contrived to have such an attack of the Gout as must at least delay his journey to Bath, if not wholly prevent it. I am persuaded the Gout is brought on or kept off at pleasure; it was the same when I wanted to join the Hamiltons to the Lakes; & three years ago, when _I_ had a fancy for Bath, nothing could induce him to have a Gouty symptom.

I have received yours, & have engaged the Lodgings in consequence. I am pleased to find that my Letter had so much effect on you, & that De Courcy is certainly your own. Let me hear from you as soon as you arrive, & in particular tell me what you mean to do with Manwaring. It is impossible to say when I shall be able to see you; my confinement must be great. It is such an abominable trick to be ill here instead of at Bath that I can scarcely command myself at all. At Bath, his old Aunts would have nursed him, but here it all falls upon me — & he bears pain with such patience that I have not the common excuse for losing my temper.

Yrs. Ever,
ALICIA.

Letter 29

Lady Susan Vernon to Mrs. Johnson.
Upper Seymour St.

My dear Alicia

There needed not this last fit of the Gout to make me detest Mr. Johnson, but now the extent of my aversion is not to be estimated. To have you confined as Nurse in his apartment! My dear Alicia, of what a mistake were you guilty in marrying a Man of his age!—just old enough to be formal, ungovernable, & to have the Gout; too old to be agreable, too young to die.

I arrived last night about five, & had scarcely swallowed my dinner when Manwaring made his appearance. I will not dissemble what real pleasure his sight afforded me, nor how strongly I felt the contrast between his person & manners & those of Reginald, to the infinite disadvantage of the latter. For an hour or two I was even staggered in my resolution of marrying him, & tho' this was too idle & nonsensical an idea to remain long on my mind, I do not feel very eager for the conclusion of my Marriage, nor look forward with much impatience to the time when Reginald, according to our agreement, is to be in Town. I shall probably put off his arrival under some pretence or other. He must not come till Manwaring is gone.

I am still doubtful at times as to Marriage. If the old Man would die, I might not hesitate; but a state of dependence on the caprice of Sir Reginald will not suit the freedom of my spirit; & if I resolve to wait for that event, I shall have excuse enough at present, in having been scarcely ten months a Widow. I have not given Manwaring any hint of my intention, or allowed him to consider my acquaintance with Reginald as more than the commonest flirtation, & he is tolerably appeased. Adieu, till we meet; I am enchanted with my Lodgings.

Yrs. ever,

S. VERNON.

Letter 30

Lady Susan Vernon to Mr. De Courcy.
Upper Seymour St.

I have received your Letter, & tho' I do not attempt to conceal that I am gratified by your impatience for the hour of meeting, I yet feel myself under the necessity of delaying that hour beyond the time originally fixed. Do not think me unkind for such an exercise of my power, nor accuse me of Instability without first hearing my reasons. In the course of my journey from Churchill, I had ample leisure for reflection on the present state of our affairs, & every review has served to convince me that they require a delicacy & cautiousness of conduct to which we have hitherto been too little attentive. We have been hurried on by our feelings to a degree of Precipitation which ill accords with the claims of our Friends or the opinion of the World. We have been unguarded in forming this hasty Engagement, but we must not complete the imprudence by ratifying it while there is so much reason to fear the Connection would be opposed by those Friends on whom you depend.

It is not for us to blame any expectations on your Father's side of your marrying to advantage; where possessions are so extensive as those of your Family, the wish of increasing them, if not strictly reasonable, is too common to excite surprise or resentment. He has a right to require a woman of fortune in his daughter in law, & I am sometimes quarrelling with myself for suffering you to form a connection so imprudent; but the influence of reason is often acknowledged too late by those who feel like me.

I have now been but a few months a widow; and, however little indebted to my Husband's memory for any happiness derived from him during a Union of some years, I cannot forget that the indelicacy of so early a second marriage must subject me to the censure of the World, & incur, what would be still more insupportable, the displeasure of Mr. Vernon. I might perhaps harden myself in time against the injustice of general reproach, but the loss of _his_ valued Esteem I am, as you well know, ill-fitted to endure; & when to this may be added the consciousness of having injured you with your Family, how am I to support myself? With feelings so poignant as mine, the conviction of having divided the son from his Parents would make me, even with _you_, the most miserable of Beings.

It will surely, therefore, be advisable to delay our Union, to delay it till appearances are more promising, till affairs have taken a more favourable turn. To assist us in such a resolution, I feel that absence will be necessary. We must not meet. Cruel as this sentence may appear, the necessity of pronouncing it, which can alone reconcile it to myself, will be evident to you when you have considered our situation in the light in which I have found myself imperiously obliged to place it. You may be—you must be—well assured that nothing but the strongest conviction of Duty could induce me to wound my own feelings by urging a lengthened separation, & of insensibility to yours you will hardly suspect me. Again, therefore, I say that we ought not, we must not yet meet. By a removal for some Months from each other, we shall tranquillize the sisterly fears of Mrs. Vernon, who, accustomed herself to the enjoyment of riches, considers Fortune as necessary everywhere, & whose Sensibilities are not of a nature to comprehend ours.

Let me hear from you soon—very soon. Tell me that you submit to my Arguments, & do not reproach me for using such. I cannot bear reproaches: my spirits are not so high as to need being repressed. I must endeavour to seek amusement abroad, & fortunately many of my Friends are in town; among them the Manwarings; you know how sincerely I regard both Husband & wife.

I am ever, Faithfully Yours
S. VERNON.

Letter 31

Lady Susan to Mrs. Johnson.
Upper Seymour St.

My dear Friend,

That tormenting creature Reginald is here. My Letter, which was intended to keep him longer in the Country, has hastened him to Town. Much as I wish him away, however, I cannot help being pleased with such a proof of attachment. He is devoted to me, heart & soul. He will carry this note himself, which is to serve as an Introduction to you, with whom he longs to be acquainted. Allow him to spend the Evening with you, that I may be in no danger of his returning here. I have told him that I am not quite well, & must be alone; & should he call again there might be confusion, for it is impossible to be sure of servants. Keep him, therefore, I entreat you, in Edward St. You will not find him a heavy companion, & I allow you to flirt with him as much as you like. At the same time do not forget my real interest; say all that you can to convince him that I shall be quite wretched if he remains here; you know my reasons—Propriety, & so forth. I would urge them more myself, but that I am impatient to be rid of him, as Manwaring comes within half an hour. Adieu,

S. V.

Letter 32

Mrs. Johnson to Lady Susan.
Edward St.

My dear Creature,

I am in agonies, & know not what to do, nor what _you_ can do. Mr. De Courcy arrived just when he should not. Mrs. Manwaring had that instant entered the House, & forced herself into her Guardian's presence, tho' I did not know a syllable of it till afterwards, for I was out when both she & Reginald came, or I should have sent him away at all events; but _she_ was shut up with Mr. Johnson, while _he_ waited in the Drawing room for me. She arrived yesterday in pursuit of her Husband; but perhaps you know this already from himself. She came to this house to entreat my Husband's interference, & before I could be aware of it, everything that you could wish to be concealed was known to him, & unluckily she had wormed out of Manwaring's servant that he had visited you every day since your being in Town, & had just watched him to your door herself! What could I do? Facts are such horrid things! All is by this time known to De Courcy, who is now alone with Mr. Johnson. Do not accuse me; indeed, it was impossible to prevent it. Mr. Johnson has for some time suspected De Courcy of intending to marry you, & would speak with him alone as soon as he knew him to be in the House.

That detestable Mrs. Manwaring, who, for your comfort, has fretted herself thinner & uglier than ever, is still here, & they have been all closeted together. What can be done? At any rate, I hope he will plague his wife more than ever.

With anxious wishes,
Yrs. faithfully
ALICIA.

Letter 33

Lady Susan to Mrs. Johnson.
Upper Seymour St.

This Eclaircissement is rather provoking. How unlucky that you should have been from home! I thought myself sure of you at 7. I am undismayed, however. Do not torment yourself with fears on my account; depend on it, I can make my story good with Reginald. Manwaring is just gone; he brought me the news of his wife's arrival. Silly woman, what does she expect by such Manoeuvres?

Yet I wish she had staid quietly at Langford. Reginald will be a little enraged at first, but by To-morrow's Dinner everything will be well again.

Adieu.
S. V.

Letter 34

Mr. De Courcy to Lady Susan.
Hotel.

I write only to bid you Farewell. The spell is removed;
I see you as you are. Since we parted yesterday, I have
received from indisputable authority such an history of
you as must bring the most mortifying conviction of
the Imposition I have been under, & the absolute necessity of an immediate & eternal separation from you.
You cannot doubt to what I allude. Langford—
Langford—that word will be sufficient. I received my
information in Mr. Johnson's house, from Mrs. Manwaring herself.

You know how I have loved you; you can intimately
judge of my present feelings; but I am not so weak as to
find indulgence in describing them to a woman who
will glory in having excited their anguish, but whose
affection they have never been able to gain.

R. DE COURCY.

Letter 35

Lady Susan to Mr. De Courcy.
Upper Seymour St.

I will not attempt to describe my astonishment in reading the note this moment received from you. I am bewildered in my endeavours to form some rational conjecture of what Mrs. Manwaring can have told you, to occasion so extraordinary a change in your sentiments. Have I not explained everything to you with respect to myself which could bear a doubtful meaning, & which the ill-nature of the World had interpreted to my Discredit? What can you _now_ have heard to stagger your Esteem for me? Have I ever had a concealment from you? Reginald, you agitate me beyond expression. I cannot suppose that the old story of Mrs. Manwaring's jealousy can be revived again, or at least be _listened_ to again. Come to me immediately, & explain what is at present absolutely incomprehensible. Believe me, the single word of _Langford_ is not of such potent intelligence as to supersede the necessity of more. If we _are_ to part, it will at least be handsome to take your personal Leave. But I have little heart to jest; in truth, I am serious enough—for to be sunk, tho' but for an hour, in your esteem is an humiliation to which I know not how to submit. I shall count every minute till your arrival.

S. V.

Letter 36

Mr. De Courcy to Lady Susan.
Hotel.

Why would you write to me? Why do you require
particulars? But since it must be so, I am obliged to
declare that all the accounts of your misconduct during
the life & since the death of Mr. Vernon, which had
reached me, in common with the World in general, &
gained my entire belief before I saw you, but which
you, by the exertion of your perverted Abilities, had
made me resolve to disallow, have been unanswerably
proved to me. Nay, more, I am assured that a connection of which I had never before entertained a thought,
has for some time existed, & still continues to exist,
between you & the Man whose family you robbed of
its Peace, in return for the hospitality with which you
were received into it! That you have corresponded
with him ever since your leaving Langford—not with
his wife—but with him—& that he now visits you
every day. Can you, dare you deny it? & all this at the
time when I was an encouraged, an accepted Lover!

From what have I not escaped! I have only to be grateful. Far from me be all complaint, & every sigh of regret. My own Folly had endangered me, my Preservation I owe to the kindness, the Integrity of another. But the unfortunate Mrs. Manwaring, whose agonies while she related the past seemed to threaten her reason—how is _she_ to be consoled?

After such a discovery as this, you will scarcely affect further wonder at my meaning in bidding you Adieu. My Understanding is at length restored, & teaches me no less to abhor the Artifices which had subdued me than to despise myself for the weakness on which their strength was founded.

R. DE COURCY

Letter 37

Lady Susan to Mr. De Courcy.
Upper Seymour St.

I am satisfied—& will trouble you no more when these few lines are dismissed. The Engagement which you were eager to form a fortnight ago is no longer compatible with your views, & I rejoice to find that the prudent advice of your Parents has not been given in vain. Your restoration to Peace will, I doubt not, speedily follow this act of filial Obedience, & I flatter myself with the hope of surviving _my_ share in this disappointment.

S. V.

Letter 38

Mrs. Johnson to Lady Susan Vernon.
Edward Street.

I am grieved, tho' I cannot be astonished, at your rupture with Mr. De Courcy; he has just informed Mr. Johnson of it by letter. He leaves London, he says, to-day. Be assured that I partake in all your feelings, & do not be angry if I say that our intercourse, even by Letter, must soon be given up. It makes me miserable; but Mr. Johnson vows that if I persist in the connection, he will settle in the country for the rest of his life—& you know it is impossible to submit to such an extremity while any other alternative remains.

You have heard of course that the Manwarings are to part, & I am afraid Mrs. M. will come home to us again; but she is still so fond of her Husband, & frets so much about him, that perhaps she may not live long.

Miss Manwaring is just come to Town to be with her Aunt, & they say that she declares she will have Sir James Martin before she leaves London again. If I were you, I would certainly get him myself. I had almost forgot to give you my opinion of Mr. De Courcy, I am really delighted with him; he is full as handsome, I think, as Manwaring, & with such an open, good-humoured countenance that one cannot help loving him at first sight. Mr. Johnson & he are the greatest friends in the World. Adieu, my dearest Susan. I wish matters did not go so perversely. That unlucky visit to Langford! But I dare say you did all for the best, & there is no defying Destiny.

Yr. sincerely attached
ALICIA.

Letter 39

Lady Susan to Mrs. Johnson.
Upper Seymour St.

My dear Alicia

I yeild to the necessity which parts us. Under circumstances you could not act otherwise. Our friendship
cannot be impaired by it, & in happier times, when
your situation is as independent as mine, it will unite
us again in the same Intimacy as ever. For this I shall
impatiently wait; & meanwhile can safely assure you
that I never was more at ease, or better satisfied with
myself & everything about me than at the present hour.
Your Husband I abhor—Reginald I despise—& I am
secure of never seeing either again. Have I not reason
to rejoice? Manwaring is more devoted to me than
ever; & were he at liberty, I doubt if I could resist even
Matrimony offered by _him_. This event, if his wife
live with you, it may be in your power to hasten. The
violence of her feelings, which must wear her out, may
be easily kept in irritation. I rely on your friendship for

this. I am now satisfied that I never could have brought myself to marry Reginald; & am equally determined that Frederica never _shall_. To-morrow I shall fetch her from Churchill, & let Maria Manwaring tremble for the consequence. Frederica shall be Sir James's wife before she quits my house. _She_ may whimper, & the Vernons may storm; I regard them not. I am tired of submitting my will to the Caprices of others; of resigning my own Judgement in deference to those to whom I owe no Duty, & for whom I feel no respect. I have given up too much, have been too easily worked on; but Frederica shall now find the difference.

Adieu, dearest of Friends. May the next Gouty Attack be more favourable! And may you always regard me as unalterably yours

S. VERNON.

Letter 40

Lady De Courcy to Mrs. Vernon.
Parklands.

My dear Catherine

I have charming news for you, & if I had not sent off my Letter this morning, you might have been spared the vexation of knowing of Reginald's being gone to Town, for he is returned, Reginald is returned, not to ask our consent to his marrying Lady Susan, but to tell us they are parted forever! He has been only an hour in the House, & I have not been able to learn particulars, for he is so very low that I have not the heart to ask questions; but I hope we shall soon know all. This is the most joyful hour he has ever given us since the day of his birth. Nothing is wanting but to have you here, & it is our particular wish & entreaty that you would come to us as soon as you can. You have owed us a visit many long weeks. I hope nothing will make it inconvenient to Mr. Vernon, & pray bring all my Grand-Children; & your dear Neice is included, of course; I long to see her.

It has been a sad, heavy winter hitherto, without Reginald, & seeing nobody from Churchill. I never found the season so dreary before; but this happy meeting will make us young again. Frederica runs much in my thoughts, & when Reginald has recovered his usual good spirits (as I trust he soon will), we will try to rob him of his heart once more, & I am full of hopes of seeing their hands joined at no great distance.

Yr. affec: Mother,

C. DE COURCY.

Letter 41

Mrs. Vernon to Lady De Courcy.
Churchill.

My dear Madam

Your Letter has surprised me beyond measure! Can it be true that they are really separated—& forever? I should be overjoyed if I dared depend on it, but after all that I have seen, how can one be secure? And Reginald really with you! My surprise is the greater because on Wednesday, the very day of his coming to Parklands, we had a most unexpected & unwelcome visit from Lady Susan, looking all chearfulness & good-humour, & seeming more as if she were to marry him when she got to London, than as if parted from him forever. She staid nearly two hours, was as affectionate & agreable as ever, & not a syllable, not a hint, was dropped of any disagreement or coolness between them. I asked her whether she had seen my Brother since his arrival in Town—not, as you may suppose, with any doubt of the fact, but merely to see how she looked. She immediately answered, without any embarrassment, that he had been kind enough to call on her on Monday, but she believed he had already returned home—which I was very far from crediting.

Your kind invitation is accepted by us with pleasure, & on Thursday next we & our little ones will be with you. Pray Heaven, Reginald may not be in Town again by that time!

I wish we could bring dear Frederica too, but I am sorry to say that her Mother's errand hither was to fetch her away; and, miserable as it made the poor Girl, it was impossible to detain her. I was thoroughly unwilling to let her go, & so was her Uncle; & all that could be urged we _did_ urge; but Lady Susan declared that as she was now about to fix herself in Town for several Months, she could not be easy if her Daughter were not with her, for Masters, &c. Her Manner, to be sure, was very kind & proper, & Mr. Vernon believes that Frederica will now be treated with affection. I wish I could think so too!

The poor girl's heart was almost broke at taking leave of us. I charged her to write to me very often, & to remember that if she were in any distress we should be always her friends. I took care to see her alone, that I might say all this, & I hope made her a little more comfortable. But I shall not be easy till I can go to Town & judge of her situation myself.

I wish there were a better prospect than now appears of the Match which the conclusion of your Letter declares your expectation of.

At present it is not very likely.

Yrs. &c.

CATH. VERNON.

Conclusion

This Correspondence, by a meeting between some of the parties, & a separation between the others, could not, to the great detriment of the Post office Revenue, be continued longer. Very little assistance to the State could be derived from the Epistolary Intercourse of Mrs. Vernon & her neice; for the former soon perceived, by the style of Frederica's letters, that they were written under her Mother's inspection, & therefore deferring all particular inquiry till she could make it personally in Town, ceased writing minutely or often.

Having learnt enough in the meanwhile from her open-hearted Brother, of what had passed between him & Lady Susan to sink the latter lower than ever in her opinion, she was proportionably more anxious to get Frederica removed from such a Mother, & placed under her own care; and, tho' with little hope of success, was resolved to leave nothing unattempted that might offer a chance of obtaining her Sister-in-law's consent to it. Her anxiety on the subject made her press for an early visit to London; & Mr. Vernon, who, as it must already have appeared, lived only to do whatever he was desired, soon found some accommodating Business to call him thither. With a heart full of the Matter, Mrs. Vernon waited on Lady Susan shortly after her arrival in Town, & was met with such an easy & chearful affection, as made her almost turn from her with horror. No remembrance of Reginald, no consciousness of Guilt, gave one look of embarrassment. She was in excellent spirits, & seemed eager to shew at once, by every possible attention to her Brother & Sister, her sense of their kindness, & her pleasure in their society.

Frederica was no more altered than Lady Susan; the same restrained Manners, the same timid Look in the presence of her Mother as heretofore, assured her Aunt of her situation's being uncomfortable, & confirmed her in the plan of altering it. No unkindness, however, on the part of Lady Susan appeared. Persecution on the subject of Sir James was entirely at an end—his name merely mentioned to say that he was not in London; & indeed, in all her conversation she was solicitous only for the welfare & improvement of her Daughter, acknowledging, in terms of grateful delight, that Frederica was now growing every day more & more what a Parent could desire.

Mrs. Vernon, surprised & incredulous, knew not what to suspect, and, without any change in her own views, only feared greater difficulty in accomplishing them. The first hope of anything better was derived from Lady Susan's asking her whether she thought Frederica looked quite as well as she had done at Churchill, as she must confess herself to have sometimes an anxious doubt of London's perfectly agreeing with her.

Mrs. Vernon, encouraging the doubt, directly proposed her Neice's returning with them into the country. Lady Susan was unable to express her sense of such kindness, yet knew not, from a variety of reasons, how to part with her Daughter; & as, tho' her own plans were not yet wholly fixed, she trusted it would ere long be in her power to take Frederica into the country herself, concluded by declining entirely to profit by such unexampled attention. Mrs. Vernon, however, persevered in the offer of it; & tho' Lady Susan continued to resist, her resistance in the course of a few days seemed somewhat less formidable.

The lucky alarm of an Influenza decided what might not have been decided quite so soon. Lady Susan's maternal fears were then too much awakened for her to think of anything but Frederica's removal from the risk of infection. Above all Disorders in the World, she most dreaded the influenza for her Daughter's constitution! Frederica returned to Churchill with her uncle & aunt; & three weeks afterwards, Lady Susan announced her being married to Sir James Martin.

Mrs. Vernon was then convinced of what she had only suspected before, that she might have spared herself all the trouble of urging a removal which Lady Susan had doubtless resolved on from the first. Frederica's visit was nominally for six weeks; but her Mother, tho' inviting her to return in one or two affectionate Letters, was very ready to oblige the whole Party by consenting to a prolongation of her stay, & in the course of two months ceased to write of her absence, & in the course of two more to write to her at all.

Frederica was therefore fixed in the family of her Uncle & Aunt till such time as Reginald De Courcy could be talked, flattered, & finessed into an affection for her—which, allowing leisure for the conquest of his attachment to her Mother, for his abjuring all future attachments, & detesting the Sex, might be reasonably looked for in the course of a Twelvemonth. Three Months might have done it in general, but Reginald's feelings were no less lasting than lively.

Whether Lady Susan was or was not happy in her second Choice—I do not see how it can ever be ascertained—for who would take her assurance of it on either side of the question? The World must judge from Probability; she had nothing against her but her Husband & her Conscience.

Sir James may seem to have drawn a harder lot than mere Folly merited. I leave him, therefore, to all the Pity that anybody can give him. For myself, I confess that _I_ can pity only Miss Manwaring, who, coming to Town & putting herself to an expense in Cloathes which impoverished her for two years, on purpose to secure him, was defrauded of her due by a Woman ten years older than herself.

FINIS

Note on the Conclusion: *What utter gibberish.*